BISHOP'S ENDGAME

ENDGAME TRILOGY

Katie Reus

Cover art: Jaycee of Sweet 'N Spicy Designs
Editor: Julia Ganis
Author website: https://www.katiereus.com

Bishop's Endgame /Katie Reus. -- 1st ed.

ISBN-13: 9781635561319
ISBN-10: 1-63556-131-0

For every single person taking it one day at a time.

Praise for the novels of Katie Reus

"Exciting in more ways than one, well-paced and smoothly written, I'd recommend *A Covert Affair* to any romantic suspense reader." —Harlequin Junkie

"Sexy military romantic suspense." —USA Today

"I could not put this book down. . . . Let me be clear that I am not saying that this was a good book *for* a paranormal genre; it was an excellent romance read, *period*." —All About Romance

"Reus strikes just the right balance of steamy sexual tension and nail-biting action....This romantic thriller reliably hits every note that fans of the genre will expect." —*Publishers Weekly*

"Prepare yourself for the start of a great new series! . . . I'm excited about reading more about this great group of characters." —Fresh Fiction

"Wow! This powerful, passionate hero sizzles with sheer deliciousness. I loved every sexy twist of this fun & exhilarating tale. Katie Reus delivers!" —Carolyn Crane, RITA award winning author

"A sexy, well-crafted paranormal romance that succeeds with smart characters and creative world building."—Kirkus Reviews

"*Mating Instinct*'s romance is taut and passionate . . . Katie Reus's newest installment in her Moon Shifter series will leave readers breathless!" —Stephanie Tyler, *New York Times* bestselling author

"You'll fall in love with Katie's heroes."
—*New York Times* bestselling author, Kaylea Cross

"Both romantic and suspenseful, a fast-paced sexy book full of high stakes action." —Heroes and Heartbreakers

"Katie Reus pulls the reader into a story line of second chances, betrayal, and the truth about forgotten lives and hidden pasts."
—The Reading Café

"Nonstop action, a solid plot, good pacing, and riveting suspense."
—RT Book Reviews

"Enough sexual tension to set the pages on fire."
—*New York Times* bestselling author, Alexandra Ivy

"...a wild hot ride for readers. The story grabs you and doesn't let go."
—*New York Times* bestselling author, Cynthia Eden

"Has all the right ingredients: a hot couple, evil villains, and a killer action-filled plot. . . . [The] Moon Shifter series is what I call Grade-A entertainment!" —Joyfully Reviewed

"*Avenger's Heat* hits the ground running...This is a story of strength, of partnership and healing, and it does it brilliantly."
—Vampire Book Club

"*Mating Instinct* was a great read with complex characters, serious political issues and a world I am looking forward to coming back to."
—All Things Urban Fantasy

PROLOGUE

Ellis Bishop gunned his engine, taking a sharp left turn. His arm muscles flexed, stretching the sleeves of his leather jacket as the motorcycle shot forward.

Faster, faster, faster, he silently urged it.

He'd found out from a source that his partner's cover had been blown and he couldn't get hold of Carter. He couldn't get hold of their boss either.

His heart thumped erratically as he took another turn, his palms damp. Only two minutes away. Two long minutes from the auto body shop where Carter was supposed to be meeting Vitaly Rodin. But an informant had alerted him that Carter's cover was blown.

And Carter would be dead upon arrival.

Not if Ellis had anything to do about it. But Carter still wasn't answering his goddamn phone.

Ellis had Bluetooth wired to his helmet so he tried again. Voicemail. Again.

Fuckfuckfuckshitfuck.

He slowed at the next red light, quickly going over his options. He couldn't park at the auto body shop—which was nothing more than a front for moving drugs and weapons. As he passed a strip of stores two blocks away from the place, he steered into the parking lot and headed around back. He parked his bike behind the dumpster of a clothing boutique that would be closed now, then jumped off, leaving his helmet behind.

He checked his phone again. No texts and no missed calls. He sent off another benign text with their code phrase letting Carter know to get out of there immediately. He'd already sent one telling him that he was starving and wanted to get pizza tonight, but he had to send another. Carter would know what it meant, if he wasn't already— *No.* He refused to even think it.

Ellis didn't know how Carter's cover had been blown, not when his cover ID was solidly built. The how and why of it was important, but now, the only thing that mattered was saving his best friend's life.

As he neared the back of the chain store that sold secondhand clothing he slowed, using one of the dumpsters as cover while he got a visual of the back of the auto body shop.

The security camera was in place above the door, angled to the right, as usual. No one was guarding the door, which wasn't completely out of the ordinary. After another scan of the back alley, he pulled a black ski mask from his pocket and tugged it on. With only a little scruff, his facial hair wasn't visible through it, and his black T-shirt, leather jacket, jeans and boots were all generic. If anyone saw him, they wouldn't be able to give a good description other than he was tall, probably white and had on biker-type clothing.

Everything was quiet as he approached the back of the shop. *Too quiet.* It was after six and dark out but there should be guards inside if their intel was anything to go on.

Withdrawing his weapon, he stayed on the opposite side of the camera as he inched closer to the back door. Jumping up, he bashed the base of the small camera with his pistol. It fell off, clattering to the concrete. He stomped on it even as he picked the lock on the door, using precious seconds to get inside. As he eased open the door, he already had his weapon up.

No one was waiting inside to jump him, but he heard muted voices coming from somewhere farther down the hallway. Faint light streamed out from the open office door ahead.

Ice slid up his spine as he slowly inched down the short hallway. The small office on the left was empty so he kept moving toward the voices coming from the four-bay garage ahead on the right.

Heart hammering in his throat, he inched down the short hallway and used his cell phone to carefully peer around the corner into the garage. From the screen he could see Carter talking to Vitaly and three others. He pressed record, wanting to get the images of all the men on video.

Ice encased his chest, wrapping around him in an un-forgiving hold. He was too late to warn Carter that Vitaly knew he was a DEA agent, but he was sure as hell going to back him up.

Before he could move, Vitaly silently, smoothly lifted a pistol and shot Carter in the chest at point-blank range. He did it so casually with absolutely no warning.

Pop. Pop. Pop.

He shot him in the head next.

Ellis reared back, watching in horror as Carter's body fell into one of the open bays. Freezing for only a moment when four other men stepped into the garage from another entryway, he knew he was outgunned. He was trained, but going up against eight men when he had one pistol and a couple extra mags? That was suicide.

That ice continued to spread, freezing his blood as he backed up, tucking the phone—the evidence—into his pocket. Moving quickly, he backtracked the way he'd come even as he locked down all his emotions. It was almost impossible, however, as grief immediately swelled up inside him, threatening to choke him.

Once he was outside, he texted his boss again, telling him quickly what had happened and to send backup to this location ASAP. Ellis and Carter had been undercover and there were only a few people he could contact at this point. Kyle Bird, his boss and mentor, was one of them.

Though he hated to leave Carter, he knew their DEA team would retrieve his body and he would receive a proper burial. It wasn't enough. Nothing would ever be enough, not with Carter dead... He bit down hard. Swallowed back the thought. He'd mourn his friend later.

As he hurried back to the dumpster, the roar of an engine rumbling through the air had him diving for cover.

Three muscle cars rolled around the corner and soon enough someone was going to see the destroyed security camera—if they didn't know about it already.

Instead of going back the way he'd come, he jumped the chain-link fence directly behind the dumpster and into a cluster of underbrush surrounding a row of palm trees common all over Orlando.

Rage building inside him, he'd started to call his boss again when his phone silently lit up. He could hear male voices coming from near the building as a car door slammed. Heart rate kicking up, he hurried into the adjacent alleyway, now sprinting in the opposite direction. There was a shout of alarm behind him, but a glance over his shoulder told him no one was giving chase. They must have just seen the camera.

Answering, he held his phone to his ear. "Carter's dead. Vitaly pulled the trigger."

Bird swore. "You're sure?"

"I saw it with my own eyes. I got a short recording on my cell phone."

Another curse. "Where are you?"

"On the move. We need to send in a team now before he goes to ground." He rattled off the address, though Bird would know it from their recon anyway. They'd been watching Vitaly and his crew for a couple months. He'd been making subtle waves in Orlando and landed on their radar because it appeared as if he was positioning himself to take over for his boss, Leonid Berezin.

They couldn't be sure though. Vitaly's movements were so precise and he was careful. Until tonight.

"I'll take care of it. Get to safety. Let me know where you are and I'll send someone to extract you."

"I will." As he raced away and circled back to his motorcycle, he emailed the short video to himself just in case something happened to him from the time he left here until he met up with Bird. He had to have a backup somewhere. When he was done, he tucked his phone back into his pocket and made his way to his bike. No one had messed with it and it was time to get out of here.

Over five hours later, he sat in a dimly lit corner booth of an all-night diner where he had a full visual of the entrance and a quick escape out the exit door. Bird was already half an hour late and had gone radio silent.

Tapping his finger against the table, Ellis didn't bother to wave the waitress away when she refilled his coffee. He'd only drunk it in an effort to warm himself up, but it hadn't worked. The little liquid he'd managed to swallow sat heavy in his gut, threatening to come up as he thought of Carter. An Army vet and loving husband—who considered himself a "grill master" yet burned every steak he cooked. The man couldn't grill for shit, but he was quick with a joke, and when Ellis had gone to him months ago and confided in him that he was getting burned out, he'd simply listened. He hadn't given bullshit advice or tried to fix anything. He'd just listened. Because that was who Carter was—or had been. He closed his eyes tight and dragged in a breath.

It took everything in him not to call Carter's wife—widow—and tell her what had happened. But he couldn't break protocol. Couldn't do anything that might put her in danger. By now Bird should have talked to her in person. Which might be why the man was late. And that was the only reason Ellis was keeping his temper in check. Not that he was angry at Bird anyway.

He was pissed at himself for being too late, for not being there in time to save Carter. If he'd just left a couple minutes earlier, drove faster, ran faster... If he hadn't bothered with the cell phone and just swept in with his weapon, maybe Carter would still be here.

What if, what if, what if. He leaned his head back against the wall, sighing. He was going to be doing the *what if* thing for a long time to come.

None of this *should* have happened, regardless. But he would deal with that and get justice for Carter.

Ellis straightened when a four-door nondescript dark green sedan pulled into the parking lot. Tensing, he almost reached for the weapon he'd tucked away in his shoulder holster, but stilled when Bird stepped out of the driver's side.

Bird looked harried, his shirt rumpled, his jacket open and a plain navy blue ball cap on his head. He pressed the key fob and strode purposefully through the front door. The little bell overhead jingled and Bird ignored the waitress as he scanned the mostly empty booths.

Relief bled into his gaze as he spotted Ellis.

"Well?" Ellis asked as Bird sat across from him. "You talked to Jessica yet?"

"Not yet. We're still wrapping up everything. Everything was as you said. You got it on video? You're sure?"

Of course he was sure. He dug out his cell phone and pulled up the video before sliding it across to Bird. "See for yourself." Ellis couldn't stomach watching it again.

Bird watched it, his eyes widening slightly. "That's a crystal clear shot of him."

Yeah, no shit. This would be enough to bring down Vitaly. He just hoped the Bureau didn't use this as leverage to bring down the bigger fish and cut Vitaly a deal. Because Carter was going to get justice. He deserved it. His wife deserved it. And Ellis wouldn't rest until his best friend's killer was locked behind bars.

Bird turned off the phone, then slid it into his windbreaker pocket.

Ellis frowned at him.

"You send this to anyone else?"

A little tingle started at the back of his neck. "No," he said quietly. He wasn't going to tell his boss that he'd sent a copy to himself.

"Good. Now stand up and put your hands up." Bird's expression was hard, his eyes a stone-cold gunmetal gray as he withdrew his weapon and trained it on Ellis.

"What are you doing?"

"You're under arrest for the murder of Carter Watson."

Son of a bitch. They were setting him up.

He wanted to deny it, but the proof was right in front of him. Instead of doing as ordered, Ellis tossed his black coffee in Bird's face and bolted out of the booth. Bird cried out even as Ellis sprinted down the short hallway that led to the two bathrooms.

Bypassing them, he kicked open the exit door as a bullet whizzed past him. He slammed the metal door behind him and grabbed a discarded broom and shoved it up under the handle.

That son of a bitch had set him up—had set Carter up and gotten him killed. Bird had to be working with Vitaly.

He would pay.

Ellis raced along the side of the building and jumped onto his bike, not looking back as he sped off. He'd have to ditch it soon because Bird would definitely track it.

He had to get to a computer, download that video and make sure it got into the right hands. Because Bird and Vitaly wouldn't get away with this.

Anyone involved with this shitstorm was going to pay. If they'd framed him for Carter's murder, they'd had hours to set him up, to set a stage. And he'd just sat back and let Bird take over because he'd trusted him. *Damn it.*

No matter what, he was going to clear his name and get justice. He just had to figure out who to trust first.

CHAPTER ONE

Present day

Arianna Stavish pushed open the side door of the Methodist church, stepping out into the crisp salt-tinged air with her friend and sponsor Sheila beside her. "Want to grab some coffee? The brew tonight was particularly awful." Which was pretty much par for the course in the AA meetings at this Miami location. For some reason the coffee was always crap, but the food tended to be amazing. Probably because women from the church donated baked goods and it was almost always homemade.

Laughing lightly, Sheila shook her head, her dark curls bouncing wildly. "No. I'm actually meeting my daughter."

Arianna's eyes widened. "That's a good thing, right?" Sheila was a recovering alcoholic like her, had been in the program for a decade, and she'd left a lot of grief and pain in her wake. She was also the first to admit that she hadn't been the best mother. Not when she was drunk anyway. And before she'd gotten sober, she'd been drunk a lot.

"Yeah, it's good, but I'm nervous. I've called my own sponsor three times this week," she said dryly.

Arianna was surprised even though she knew that Sheila had a sponsor. Of course she did. It was just that she went to Sheila for advice about so many things, and the other woman was so steady and sometimes seemed all-knowing. Which was ridiculous. Just like Arianna, she would always be a recovering alcoholic. The fun disease that never went away. No matter how much she wished it would.

But that wasn't the right kind of thinking so she shelved that thought. "I'm glad for you," she said, leaning in for a hug. "Let me know if you change your mind about Christmas, okay?" She'd been invited to a friend's place for Christmas and had been told to bring friends if she wanted. One of the teachers where she taught had decided to skip traveling for the holidays and was having a big blowout at her house for all those without immediate family in the area. Luckily not everyone she worked with drank, so she'd be able to blend in and relax.

"I will."

"Good luck tonight."

"Thanks." Sheila smiled, her expression one of nerves intermingled with excitement.

Arianna was glad for her friend. Unlike Sheila, she hadn't hurt any family members with her drinking. No, she'd just hurt herself. A lot. Drinking had been her way of coping with...everything. Fat lot of good it had done her. She was just lucky she'd gotten her shit together before she'd totally destroyed her life—and she reminded herself of that every day.

She didn't want to travel back down that dark path ever again. The escape drinking had provided had been temporary and simply an illusion. Because once the numbness had worn off, the pain had still been there. Alcohol didn't make it go away—it only helped her to make even worse decisions.

As Arianna headed for her car, she realized she'd left the little gift Sheila had given her inside their meeting room. Inwardly cursing her own forgetfulness, she headed back into the church, her shoes squeaking softly against the linoleum. She'd been in Alcoholics Anonymous for the last three years, and while she didn't buy into most of the religious aspect of all of it, she'd formed close bonds with a small group of people here. And those relationships, the support, that was what had saved her life.

She hurried past the half-open door of a grief group that met here at the same time AA did and tugged the door shut on her way. It looked as if they were all still meeting and she didn't want them to be disturbed. There was also a Narcotics Anonymous meeting down the hall but they met on Mondays and Wednesdays.

She ducked into the room, intending to grab the little bag then get out, but stopped when she saw one of the old-timers folding up chairs by himself.

"Hey, Aaron." She tucked the gift bag into her purse and set it on the floor before picking up one of the metal chairs that was probably from the seventies. "You're not supposed to be doing this tonight." The regulars alternated and it wasn't his turn.

He laughed as he bent over, his patch-covered leather vest riding up. "Don't I know it. But someone's got to put these up or we'll hear about it later."

"I'll help and we'll knock this out faster."

He simply nodded and grabbed another chair.

In his sixties, Aaron was one of the first people who'd approached her at her first meeting. He'd been a friendly face in a sea of strangers. While they weren't exactly friends, more acquaintances than anything else, she knew his "story," just as he knew most of hers. They were all fairly open in these groups, though she'd never given all of the details of what had driven her to drink. There were some things she kept close to her heart, because they were etched into her soul. The knowledge hers, and hers alone.

But she'd been honest about the death of her mother and then her younger brother, practically back to back. The only person she'd ever told about the other reason that had sent her into a dark spiral of out-of-control drinking was Sheila. Because Arianna trusted and loved her. And it had taken her a year before she'd told her sponsor everything.

She shook that thought off, however. Right now she didn't want to get caught up in the past, in things she couldn't change. She'd found that if she didn't focus on the present and moving forward, she would start to spiral.

School had just let out for the next two and a half weeks, and as a teacher she was excited about the Christmas break. It was a time to spend with friends, relax and enjoy her hobbies. Christmas was a hard time for her now that her mom and brother were gone so she stayed busy and surrounded herself with people who were positive. "Any big plans for Christmas?" she asked Aaron as she grabbed two more chairs and folded them up.

Unlike many of the members in this group, Aaron hadn't lost his family to drinking. His wife had taken him back once he finally got sober. Then he'd eventually patched up his relationship with his kids. Now he was a doting grandfather whose grandkids adored and called him Poppy, but he still went to meetings twice a week. He was an inspiration to so many of them.

His presence was also a reminder that these meetings were always going to be part of her life, part of who she was. She never wanted to get to the point where she thought she didn't need them. Because she knew what happened when she slacked off and gave in to the temptation to try "just one drink." She kept going until she blacked out her memories and woke up in a bed not her own. Or not in a bed at all, but in the driver's seat of her car, parked at a local shopping center with no memory of how she'd gotten there. She shuddered, tucking away that awful memory, thankful she hadn't harmed anyone with her reckless behavior. It was one of her recurring nightmares—that she'd actually hurt someone else while trying to chase away her own demons.

"Yes indeed, my wife surprised me with a cruise this year. I'm not too keen on the idea, but I figure if she took my sorry ass back, I can smile and go on the cruise.

Though I figure it'll be a good time because she's usually right about everything..."

She was silent as he talked about his plans, happy to listen as they cleaned up the room. Aaron was definitely a talker, and while sometimes it could be a bit much, he had a big heart and was one of the most non-judgmental people she'd ever met. He owned all of his mistakes with no excuses thrown in for good measure. It was incredibly rare to meet someone like that and she appreciated his bluntness.

As they finished up, a skinny man with jeans hanging off his hips who couldn't be more than twenty years old stepped into the room, his hands shoved into the raggedy pockets. He looked around, his expression tense. "Is this the NA meeting?"

Aaron stepped forward without missing a beat. "Sorry, son, this is AA. NA is on Mondays and Wednesdays..."

She grabbed her purse as Aaron took over, ready to get out of there. Aaron had that whole grandfatherly thing going on and she knew he would very likely drive the guy to an NA meeting across town that met tonight.

She stepped out into the cool night air, glancing over at the lights from the nearby nativity scene. The whole church was lit up outside but the parking lot itself was dimly lit, and she realized the light from the pole above her car had burned out sometime during the meeting.

"Are you freaking kidding me?" she muttered to herself. She was tempted to go back inside and ask Aaron to walk her to her car but she pulled out her pepper spray and steeled herself for the walk across the nearly empty parking lot. She couldn't live in fear, couldn't spiral back down that dark hole again. She couldn't be afraid to walk to her car or go get groceries by herself because she was afraid of being jumped in the parking lot. She'd lived with that fear and it had nearly eaten her up from the inside. Made her afraid of her own shadow until she'd been a barely functioning shell. She was still cautious—she was a single woman in a huge city so she wasn't stupid. But she refused to let that fear take over her life.

Her heart rate increased, her breathing shallow as she quickly hurried across the pavement. Key fob in hand, she shoved out a breath of relief as she slid into the driver's seat, locking the doors immediately behind her. That was what one of her self-defense instructors had taught her, to immediately lock her doors once she got inside her car. Always and without exception. She'd taken the lesson to heart and did it on instinct now.

"Start the car and drive west out of the parking lot."

The deep male voice from behind her made her scream but it was quickly cut off as he pressed a gun to her bare neck.

"No screaming. Start the car."

Her fingers turned to ice as she sat there in the cool interior, looking in the rearview mirror to see a man wearing a mask. In the darkness she could barely make out anything, not even his eyes. Just that his mask was black and that he had a gun to her neck.

Instead of starting her car, she dropped her keys to the floorboard. "No." He could just kill her here. She'd been raped before. She wasn't going to drive herself to a fate like that.

He paused and shoved the gun against her head. "I don't think you understand me."

"I understand you. Shoot me now." She wasn't getting dragged somewhere else where he could do God only knew what to her. That was another lesson she'd learned in self-defense. If someone tried to take you, better to let them injure you instead of taking you somewhere. They were more likely to just flee than try to deal with a fighter. She'd learned a lot of things about herself in the last few years and she wasn't driving herself to her own rape and murder.

"Pick up those keys."

"No!" She started screaming as she reached for the door handle, well aware of the gun pressing into her. She couldn't take on a man with a gun but she could scream for attention. She yanked on the locked door as she continued screaming, even as she mentally prepared for him to shoot her.

If it was in the head, she wouldn't feel it and should be dead within a minute. She bit back a sob at the thought, because she didn't want to die. She'd overcome so much. There was so much she still wanted to do and see.

He cursed under his breath as she tugged the door open, clapping a hand over her mouth. She struggled against the sweet smell even as blackness engulfed her.

CHAPTER TWO

A rianna opened her eyes slowly, blinking into... The dimly lit bedroom.

My bedroom.

Her heart kicked wildly against her chest as she stared in horror at a strange man sitting with his back to her. At her small, neat desk, her laptop was open in front of him, the bright light from the screen illuminating his masked face. She tried to shift but her wrists and ankles were tied to her chair.

"Good, you're awake," he growled at her without turning around.

Throat tight, she couldn't respond even if she'd been able to around the gag. What were they doing at her house? She swallowed back bile as she thought of the many reasons he could have brought her here. All of them horrific. How had he known where she lived? Questions punched through her mind even as she yanked on the flex ties. They dug into her wrists and ankles as she tried to thrash around.

He pushed back from her chair and it made a dangerous creaking sound under his weight. The guy was huge, sending even more spirals of fear winding through her as he turned toward her. She swallowed hard and looked away, desperate to give in to her flight response. But she couldn't move, and the fear of death—or worse—threatened to choke her.

Out of the corner of her eye, she could see his hand coming toward her face and flinched instinctively.

His hand froze in midair.

"I'm taking your gag out. If you scream, it goes right back on. Understand?" His voice was deep.

She nodded. Even if she did scream, the neighbors to her left were out of town for the next week and a half on a Caribbean cruise, and the neighbor to the right was likely already in bed and wore hearing aids. No one would hear her unless some random passerby was out walking their dog. Considering how cold it was and that it was well after dark, she doubted it.

As he pulled the gag out, she tensed, waiting for...anything.

"What's your password?" He'd already turned away from her, dismissing her as if she was a non-threat.

Considering that her arms and legs were tied to a chair and he likely weighed double what she did and was armed, he wasn't wrong. But if she could get away, she could run. She might not be a physical match for this guy but she was pretty sure she could outrun him. Or maybe bash him in the head with something if she could just get her hands free.

"Password," he growled out again.

"What?" she asked dumbly, jumping at the sound of his voice.

He turned, her chair creaking again. "What is the password to your computer?" This time he spoke slowly, as if she was stupid.

She gritted her teeth. What did he want on her computer? She didn't have anything sensitive on her laptop and couldn't imagine what he wanted on it. But she wasn't going to die over a password so she gave it to him. As soon as she did, he turned away from her once again.

She wiggled her wrists, trying to get some space so she could slide them out, but the bindings dug into her wrists with no give. Tears pricked her eyes as she struggled, but she fought back a sob building in her throat.

"I wouldn't bother if I were you. You're just going to bruise up your wrists." He didn't even look her way, could likely hear her. "And my partner is waiting outside. There's nowhere to run."

He had a partner? That sinking feeling in her gut tightened even more. What did he want? Or what did they want? And who were "they"? Bile rose up again in a swift rush but she pushed it back down because she wasn't throwing up on herself right now. Maybe later, but she needed to keep her shit together as long as she could, figure out what to do.

He was quiet as he clicked away on her laptop. Then he plugged a small USB into the side of it and some weird-looking program popped up.

She frowned at the screen, and even though she didn't want to draw attention to herself she said, "I'm just a teacher. I don't make much money."

He simply snorted, then turned and looked at her. "A third-grade teacher is quite the cover."

"What cover?" she asked, not sure what he meant.

His blue eyes were visible even with the mask as he watched her intently, as if trying to figure her out. "How do you like the Cayman Islands?"

She blinked at the random question. "I've never been. Why have you kidnapped me? Why are we at my house? And what are you looking for on my computer? If you tell me, I can give it to you." The fact that he was still wearing a mask was the only thing that gave her a teeny tiny sliver of hope in her heart right now. Because if he had on a mask, it meant he didn't want her to see his face. Which might mean that he planned to let her go. At least that was what she'd learned from all the crime shows and detective books she read. But maybe... God, who knew anything right now?

He simply sat there watching her, barely blinking. "You were just there a month ago."

She snorted. "The hell I was." She took little weekend trips, usually diving or boating somewhere off the Florida coast, but she scheduled her vacations during summers and other school breaks. She hadn't taken any vacation a month ago. Not to mention, she'd freaking remember if she'd been to the Caymans! What was wrong with this guy?

He sat there watching her for a long moment, then turned at the sound of a soft pinging coming from her computer. When he faced the screen again, she shoved out a breath. It wasn't like she should be relieved or anything because she was still a captive, but when he'd been watching her with that intense gaze, she felt as if she'd been under a microscope.

She shifted in her seat slightly as her bladder protested. Oh God, not now. *No, no, no.* She squeezed her thighs together, willing herself to take in slow, steady breaths. She'd had too much coffee at the AA meeting and now she was paying for it. Maybe if she peed herself he wouldn't rape her? Not if she was covered in urine. Or maybe that would just enrage him. Or turn him on. Ugh, what should she do?

He pulled out the USB and turned to look at her. Even with the mask, she could see his dawning expression. "You have to pee?" he asked, all businesslike.

Fighting the terror working its way through her, she simply nodded.

"I'm going to cut your wrists and ankles free. If you try to fight me I will hogtie you and let you wet yourself. Understand?"

She simply nodded and fought the tears welling up. So maybe he didn't care if she peed on herself. Tears flooded her eyes anyway and he frowned when he saw them. As if her tears offended him. *Well excuse me, Mr. Kidnapper.* He was lucky she wasn't a sobbing mess right now.

"Save your bullshit tears," he growled as more of them spilled over.

They weren't bullshit, but screw him. She sniffed once and clamped down hard as he cut the ties. She flinched as he cut them free, afraid he'd accidentally cut her.

She had a fantasy of kicking him in the balls and then knocking him unconscious but she knew that wasn't happening. She would maybe get two feet before he jumped on her and pinned her to the ground. Then she would pee all over herself and him. *Ugh.* And right now she was concentrating on not making him angry. If she could figure out what he wanted—if it was anything other than rape and murder—maybe she could give it to him.

"Come on," he said, grabbing her upper arm surprisingly gently. He stayed glued to her as they walked to her bathroom. "Door stays open," he said as she stepped inside.

She hesitated, not wanting to take off any article of clothing with him standing there. Not that it mattered. If he wanted to... *Nope.* She was not letting her mind go there or she would completely freeze up and then have a breakdown. If that happened, she'd be having a full-blown panic attack.

He turned to the side, looking away though she knew he had a visual of her in his peripheral.

She hated this, but it would have to do. Feeling beyond awkward, the sensation mixing in with her terror, she tugged her pants down. She closed her eyes, fighting back more tears as she quickly took care of business.

She was surprised that he stood there as she washed her hands and dried them, not saying a word. Letting her hands fall to her side, she stood there staring at him, unsure what else to do. "What do you want from me?"

"You're going to pack a small bag and then we're leaving."

"No," she snapped. "I'm not going anywhere with you." It was a stupid thing to say but the words were out before she could stop herself. She'd been helpless before and she hated this feeling. Hated everything about this. It was almost worse now because she was stone-cold sober. Did she have some kind of homing beacon that attracted insane people? Monsters? She'd been a victim before and had sworn she never would be again. Unfortunately life didn't work like that. All the self-defense classes in the world weren't going to help her against this giant man with a gun and knife.

He scrubbed a hand over his masked face. "You're coming with me whether you like it or not. Your father took something from me and he's going to pay."

Oh God, this was some kind of weird vendetta against her stepfather? "He's my stepfather," she whispered, wrapping her arms around herself. "Just tell me what you want. He'll pay." Or she was pretty sure he would. She wasn't close to Vitaly, not really. After her mother had died, then her half-brother, she and her stepfather didn't see each other often. She wasn't even planning on going over to his place for Christmas this year, choosing to spend it with friends instead. And he only lived in Orlando, not that far from Miami.

Though at that thought, she wondered if she would even make it to Christmas, or even tomorrow morning.

The way things were looking... *No.* She wasn't going to let her head go in that direction. She was going to get through this.

"Come on," he ordered, stepping back so she could walk out of the bathroom.

She turned sideways as she moved past him, careful not to touch him anywhere. It wasn't like she had any control but she wasn't going to touch the guy unless she had to.

Inside her bedroom she stood there staring at one of her bookshelves, feeling lost and out of sorts. Everything looked foreign to her, from her closed bamboo blinds and the sheer gray drapes that fell over them to the white and pale lavender pin-tuck comforter set. It was as if she was looking at something that wasn't hers.

"Pack enough for a few days."

A few days? She swallowed hard as she tried to focus on his words, to think about where her overnight bag was. As she stepped toward her closet, she remembered that her stepfather had given her a gun. She'd never used it, but he'd been insistent so she'd tucked it away in her closet. It was in a little lockbox and the key was in her nightstand.

She turned toward her nightstand and she swore he must have read her mind because he said, "I've got your little twenty-two special, so don't even think about going for the key."

Any sense of hope she had fled at his words. Swallowing hard she pulled out a little duffel bag covered in dancing unicorns.

He frowned as she put the bag on the bed.

"What?" she whispered, unable to fight the trembles rolling through her—and barely pushing back the nausea.

He didn't respond, just looked at her then at the bag in a sort of confused state.

He didn't like unicorns? Well screw him. She didn't like being kidnapped.

Arianna moved quickly, grabbing random pieces from her closet. She had no idea where he was taking her, or what he really wanted other than revenge against her stepfather. Would he torture her to get back at her stepfather? When she went to open her underwear drawer, she paused then looked at him. She didn't want him seeing all her intimate things; it made her feel even more vulnerable.

He snapped to attention and pushed her aside to peer in the drawer.

"Oh…" Clearing his throat, he stepped back as if the sight of her underwear made him uncomfortable.

She grabbed a bundle and shoved them in the bag without looking at anything she'd taken or at him. "How'd you get in my house? I have an alarm system." She knew she probably shouldn't push, but she wanted to know. He'd kidnapped her but she'd been passed out when they'd gotten here. And she knew she'd turned her alarm system on when she left for her meeting. She always did.

He paused, as if he wasn't going to answer. Then, to her surprise he said, "I used your thumbprint to open your phone, then disabled your security system from the app. You should have had a lock on the app."

She blinked at his tone and words. She'd set up the app so that she didn't have to type in the damn code every time because her phone itself had a lock. Oh God, she wanted to kick herself.

But she couldn't think like that. She had to escape, had to get away. To get help. Otherwise she was definitely going to end up with a bullet in her head.

CHAPTER THREE

Ellis pulled into the garage of his safe house, very aware of the tied-up woman on the floorboards behind him. Bringing her here was a risk but she was the weakest link in the organization. And he was going to use her to his advantage—use her against her father.

Her tears had bothered him earlier, and he could admit that he didn't like using a woman this way. But he was going to get his life back and he was going to make sure Carter's killer went to jail.

She was dirty just like her father, using her cover as a schoolteacher to hide all of her ugly deeds. When he'd been working with his team for the DEA, she'd only been a name in a file. She'd hadn't been important to them because as far as they'd known she'd had nothing to do with her father's operations. They'd assumed she had no knowledge. So she'd been firmly off their radar.

Now he knew differently. Because someone from his team, his boss if he had to guess, had covered up her involvement somehow. It was the only thing that made sense. Because Ellis had recently discovered offshore bank accounts in her name with millions of dollars in them.

An elementary school teacher didn't make millions of dollars to begin with, and even considering the trust her mother had left her—Arianna didn't have close to that much money. So the fact that she was funneling millions offshore was very bad. And now he was going to get his answers. He was done hiding, done running for something he hadn't done. He was going to use her to pull Vitaly out into the open, then crush him and his corrupt organization.

Once the garage door closed behind him, he jumped out of the vehicle and opened the back door. He'd tied up Arianna's hands and had a cover over her head so she wouldn't know where he'd taken her. He pulled it off and she blinked a couple times before glaring up at him.

"Sit up," he ordered.

She struggled to sit upright in the cramped space and he resisted the urge to help her. It went against everything in his nature to treat a woman like this. But if he didn't stop her father from his ultimate plan, Ellis knew the man was going to release lethal designer drugs all over Miami and take over the criminal organization he was currently just a middleman in.

Back when Ellis had been investigating Vitaly's boss, Leonid Berezin, they'd discovered that Vitaly had been working with a chemist located in the Dominican Republic without his boss's knowledge. It was a bold move, sneaky and treacherous and not at all surprising. Most of his operations were based out of Orlando but he'd been coming to Miami where his stepdaughter lived more and more. And they'd been almost certain that his next move was to flood the streets here. But first, Ellis was certain that Vitaly would take out, or attempt to take out, Berezin.

Despite himself, Ellis helped Arianna get out of the SUV since it was so high up.

She wrenched her arms away from him the moment her feet touched the concrete floor. Hate lingered in her eyes, the most beautiful, bright green eyes he'd ever seen. They seemed even brighter against her bronze skin. Her long, dark hair was down around her face in soft waves.

A pretty little monster was what she was. She even looked innocent, with those big, beguiling eyes and her petite, soft body. Under normal circumstances, she would have been his type even if she was only twenty-five. As it was, she was going to jail if he had anything to say about it. Even if she wasn't directly involved in the day-to-day operations of her stepfather, she was still helping her stepfather by hiding his money.

Though to look at her house or her shopping habits you would never know she had millions tucked away. He'd been watching her the last couple weeks, looking for weaknesses and habits, and he'd seen her pick up a few furniture pieces at consignment shops. She then took them home, refurbished them and sold them for a small profit. It was odd, but a damn good cover for the reality of her financial situation. She'd even won teacher of the year last year so she was really playing up her role to perfection.

He guided her through to the mudroom, turned the alarm off, then reset it. "I picked this place because it has no neighbors. You can scream all you want."

Taking him off guard, she did just that, screaming her head off and making him wince.

Shaking his head, he opened the other door into the kitchen even as she continued screaming bloody murder. "Jesus, no one can hear you, but it's annoying. I'm going to gag you if you don't stop."

"You told me to scream," she muttered.

"Yeah, well, don't do it again." He glanced down at her as they stepped into the kitchen.

She was looking around curiously but the fear was definitely there. Good. He needed her afraid so she would cooperate with him.

"Here's what we're going to do. You're going to be accommodating and—"

She kicked him in the knee before racing away in the direction of the garage.

"Shit." Ignoring the bite of pain in his leg, he rounded the center island and stopped her before she could escape the kitchen.

Eyes wide, she punched at him as best she could, but he wrapped his arms around her to take away her leverage and pinned her against the quartz countertop.

"I don't want to hurt you. Stop thrashing around," he gritted out.

"If you think I'm going to be accommodating while you rape me—"

"Jesus!" He jerked back, stunned, but didn't let go of her. Of course she would be afraid of that. She was a woman and he'd kidnapped her. *Fuuuuuuuck.* "That's not what this is about. I said accommodating because you're going to sit here and listen to what I have to say."

Breathing hard, she stared up at him, glaring daggers, and he knew that if she'd had her hands free and a weapon, she wouldn't hesitate to use it.

It bothered him on a very deep level that she was afraid he would sexually assault her. He glanced away from her, unable to look into those angry eyes as he guided her to one of the seats at the island top. He moved quickly and secured her hands again because he wasn't going to take a chance that she'd try to run. She wouldn't get far but he didn't feel like chasing her down and he didn't want to accidentally hurt her.

"Your stepfather took something of mine." Technically her stepfather had killed his best friend and stolen Ellis's life. "You're going to help me get my life back. We're going to take a trip down to the Cayman Islands—"

She started laughing almost maniacally. "You're out of your freaking mind if you think I'm going to willingly get on an airplane with you—"

"And you are going to withdraw all of your dirty money," he finished in a flat tone.

She gaped at him. "Are you high? I don't have any money in the Cayman Islands. I'm a freaking teacher! And yes, I know my stepfather makes a lot of money but that doesn't mean I have any of it. Even the money my mom left me is in a trust and I don't get it until I'm twenty-eight. If you want to ransom me, you're going to have to ask him for the money. I don't have access to any of his accounts," she snapped. While she didn't call him a dumbass, it was clear from her expression that was exactly what she thought he was.

Damn, she was a really good liar. He flipped open two of the folders he'd left on the countertop. "Lie all you want. But this doesn't." He slid one folder in front of her and turned to the first page.

She looked down at the bank account statements and frowned, "What is this?"

"You tell me. It's your money."

Frowning, she looked down again, reading more thoroughly. "Can you let one of my hands go?" she murmured as she leaned down, trying to get a better look at everything. He released one of her wrists and she started flipping the pages, faster and faster. "This doesn't make any sense. It's my name, but it has to be someone with the same name..."

She trailed off, probably because she realized how ridiculous that sounded since there was a picture of her photo ID in the file as well.

"Hey! How did they get this," she shouted more to herself than him. "And that's my signature!" Now she was indignant. She reached for the other file folder and started flipping through those papers as well. "This is ridiculous." Shaking her head, she finally looked up at him. "This isn't my money. I don't know what all this is, but it's not mine."

"Sure, and you didn't go down to the Cayman Islands a month ago to make a hefty deposit." He tapped his finger against a copy of the plane tickets. God, she was so convincing—so damn beautiful, and it annoyed the shit out of him. His partner was dead and she was lying straight to his face.

"I didn't," she snapped, looking at the copies of her plane E-tickets. "Wait a minute," she muttered, flipping over the papers again. "I wasn't anywhere near the Cayman Islands for these dates, and I can prove it."

He snorted.

"I'm serious. If you just give me a computer—"

Now he was the one who laughed. Yeah, he'd just give her internet access, no problem. Now who was out of their mind?

She rolled her eyes. "Fine. Use your phone or computer or whatever and I'll tell you what to look up. I was at a teacher's association function up in Tampa. It was a big to-do, a gala that took place on this Friday night." She pointed to the date of the first plane ticket. "And at the time of this flight, I was definitely in Tampa. By chance I was sitting near the podium and I ended up in a bunch of the pictures because of the location of my seat. I had no idea until later, until some of my friends who hadn't been there told me they liked my dress. Look it up. It's all over the association's website and a local paper in Tampa. And early the next morning, I ran a 10K for breast cancer awareness." She rattled off the name of the sponsor. "Look on their Facebook page. Maybe even Instagram. I'm in a bunch of pictures at the finish line and my friend tagged me in a few. I never got any pictures myself, but there are plenty of me online."

Frowning, he did as she said and found all the images. He was quiet for a long moment as he digested this news, the lead ball in his gut expanding. He had to do more re-search, to make sure this was real. "Did you tell your stepfather about your travel plans? About the gala?"

"I don't think so. I mean, I could have but probably not. We don't talk much. And since it's pretty clear you've been stalking me you should know that!"

"Those bank accounts are still yours."

She let out a frustrated growl. "If I had millions of dollars, do you think I would be living in my cute little cottage?" she snapped. Then she shook her head. "Scratch that, because I probably would be. I love that house, but whatever. Those aren't my accounts. But sure, let's go to the Cayman Islands and I'll get all that money out for you," she tossed at him as if he was crazy.

Right about now, he was feeling it. He'd been so damn sure she was embedded with her father. Maybe she still was. But...he was really good at weeding out liars. His very life depended on it, especially when he'd gone undercover. And from what he could tell she'd been truly shocked to see these bank accounts. If these pictures were real, if she had been in the States for both of these events, he couldn't see how she could have flown down to the Cayman Islands and gotten back so quickly. Not possible.

He tapped his finger against the countertop, then stopped. "Come on." He released her other wrist and motioned for her to stand.

"Where are you taking me?" Fear laced her words, was evident in her eyes even as she stared up at him defiantly—and it ate at his insides.

If he was wrong about her and he'd kidnapped an in-nocent woman… *No.* She was in this up to her eyeballs. She had to be.

He led her to the attached living room and she sat while he picked up his laptop. Ellis worked quickly on his computer, looking over the images again and thor-oughly checking out the social media pages of the organ-izations. He hadn't found them before because they hadn't been on her social media page directly—and he had definitely been monitoring her stuff.

Arianna was quiet as he worked, digging even deeper into her life. He'd thought he had everything he needed but the more he dug, the heavier that sinking sensation in his gut grew. One of his former confidential inform-ants had given him the tip on Arianna, but now…

Now he was wondering how good this was at all. The bank accounts and the other information pointed in her direction but she was so genuinely surprised and indig-nant. And she'd never been on their radar back when he'd been with the administration.

What if his former CI had lied? And what if this was all some sort of ploy by her stepfather for…something Ellis wasn't seeing? *Damn it.* He rubbed a hand over his face, annoyed by the stupid mask.

"Get up," he said.

She jerked slightly in surprise as his voice broke through the silence of the room, fear clear in her eyes as she stood. "What are we doing?"

"You're going to get some sleep." He'd been burning it hard for the last forty-eight hours and he needed a couple hours of sleep. Maybe his head would be clearer in the morning and he would see what he was missing.

She narrowed her gaze at him.

He gently took her elbow and guided her up the stairs. The scent of her lavender and mint soap teased the air, soft and subtle. "In here." He dropped her duffel bag on the bed. "Change into pajamas if you want. You've got two minutes."

He shut the door to give her some privacy. He'd made sure the windows were secure and there was no way she could get out of the small bathroom window regardless.

He looked at his watch, and after a minute and a half he opened the door to find her wearing pajamas covered in little hearts, sitting on the end of the bed, her arms wrapped tightly around herself.

Shit. If she really was innocent, he was going to feel like the biggest douche in the world. Worse than. Part of him wanted to apologize, to tell her that if she ended up not being tied to her monster of a stepfather, that he truly was sorry for what he'd done. But if she was guilty, he didn't want to show any weakness. And he'd learned the hard way that when monsters sensed weakness, they'd twist the knife until you were dead.

No, she needed to think he was ruthless enough to do anything.

"I'm going to secure one of your hands to the headboard."

Stark terror flared in her eyes and he looked away, unable to meet her gaze.

"I'm not going to hurt you. I just need sleep and I'm not going to risk you sneaking out or knocking me out."

"What about your partner?" Her voice vibrated with fear.

He looked at her again and cleared his throat.

Understanding dawned in her gaze. "You lied? It's just you?"

He lifted a shoulder.

She gritted her teeth, glaring at him as he snapped a new flex tie to the headboard, then snapped one around her wrist, connecting them.

Next he cuffed them together as he stretched out on the opposite side of the bed.

She stared at him for a long moment then rolled onto her side, giving him her back. It pulled his arm into an uncomfortable position, but he figured he probably deserved it at this point.

He was a light sleeper but he hadn't wanted to take the chance that she would escape the headboard while he was out. And if they were cuffed together, there was no way that was happening.

"You're an asshole," she muttered as she tried to get comfortable.

"I've been called worse."

"Oh, I have no doubt about that," she snapped. "So did you find those pictures? Did you see that I'm telling the truth?"

He stared up at the ceiling, his arm stretched out at an uncomfortable angle. "I saw the pictures."

"Well?"

"Well nothing."

She let out a growl of frustration and flopped onto her back so that their arms lay between them. "Those aren't my accounts no matter what you say."

"Well if they're not your accounts, then someone went to a lot of trouble to make it look like they are. Why do you think that is?" He'd used an old contact to help him get those records but now... He knew he was going to have to reach out to someone he genuinely liked, someone with ties to his "real life," someone he didn't want to involve in this shit. But he had no choice. Months had passed and he wasn't making as much progress as he should be.

Out of the corner of his eye he saw Arianna frown, then bite her bottom lip as she digested his statement. Then she sniffed haughtily. "I'm not believing anything you say, Mr. *Kidnapper.*" She turned away from him again and to his surprise she fell into a light sleep barely fifteen minutes later.

Maybe it wasn't surprising though. She'd been through a shock tonight with being kidnapped and her adrenaline would be crashing hard. Shit, he hadn't even fed her, he realized. Though to be fair, he hadn't eaten either.

Recently food hadn't been important. Staying alive and trying to find the truth were paramount. He'd thought he would find it tonight with her, that he'd be that much closer to bringing Vitaly to him.

Now he found himself questioning his decision to take her. Maybe kidnapping Arianna Stavish hadn't been the smartest decision after all.

CHAPTER FOUR

"Hey...Kidnapper!" Arianna's annoyed voice carried through from the next room.

Ellis pushed his laptop to the side and stood, heading to the bedroom immediately to find her twisting against the sheets, kicking at them in frustration as she yanked on the one wrist still flex-cuffed to the headboard.

"I've got to...use the facilities," she growled at him. This morning there was no fear in her eyes, just a whole lot of annoyance.

He shut down his guilt at seeing her like this and quickly released her wrists. Then he grabbed her bag from the floor as she stood. "Take a shower too if you want." There was nowhere for her to go in there.

She snatched the bag out of his hand and hurried into the bathroom, slamming it with wall-shaking force. Oh yeah, she'd moved into pure anger territory and he didn't blame her. The fear would be back once she'd woken up a little more, but for now she was pissed. He preferred anger to the fear.

He hadn't been able to sleep long next to her, but he'd grabbed a few hours of rest at least, and for the last three hours he'd been digging even deeper into her background. As much as he could with his limited resources. But he was now fairly sure his former CI had lied to him. Which was what he got for trusting someone with a lengthy criminal background. And he had no way to go after the guy for his lies either. He couldn't go to his former boss—the traitor.

Ellis was also pretty sure that someone had directed the CI to lie, though he wasn't sure why. Because the information he had on the bank accounts was real. But the deeper he looked, something about the way the accounts had been set up—and when—was all off. So it seemed clear that someone had wanted him to go after Arianna. But why? To throw him off the right trail, maybe?

Unfortunately there was only so much he could do on his own. He'd always relied on a team and tech-savvy analysts to do all the digging while he'd done what he was good at. Undercover work with assholes.

At the sound of the shower starting, he sat on the edge of the bed because he was pretty sure Arianna was going to try to run again. He'd be surprised if she didn't try.

He looked at his watch and started timing her. Sixty seconds passed before the door creaked open.

Arianna peeked out, her expression tight. When she saw him sitting on the bed, she let out a growl of frustration then slammed the door again. This time he heard the rustle of the shower curtain and knew she was actually getting inside.

As he sat there, one of his burner phones buzzed in his pocket. He recognized the number and answered immediately. "Yeah?"

"Is this who I think it is?" a familiar female voice tentatively asked.

He allowed himself a small sigh of relief. He'd left a vague message, hoping she understood the code. "Yes."

"What took you so long to reach out to me?" Lizzy Caldwell shouted at him.

He winced slightly. He'd known Lizzy—hacker extraordinaire—for ages, and though they'd taken different career paths, they ran in a lot of the same circles. And she was also friends with his brother-in-law and brother. "I didn't want to get you in trouble for having contact with me. Even you can't talk your way out of working with a wanted felon. It's called accessory after the fact. And there are some really dangerous people involved in this mess."

She snorted as if he was completely stupid. "That's bullshit."

"Maybe so, but I wasn't going to put a friend in danger. Your husband would have killed me himself if I'd done that."

She sniffed slightly. "Fine. I'll just kick your ass later—and you're not wrong about Porter. Anyway, I got your cryptic message. What's going on?"

He certainly wasn't going to tell her that he'd kidnapped someone, so he cleared his throat. "I need you to dig deep on a woman named Arianna Stavish. Her stepfather is Vitaly Rodin." She'd never taken the guy's name, something Ellis found interesting.

"I know his name, not hers," she murmured and he could hear the soft sound of fingers moving over a keyboard in the background.

"Look, what I'm asking you to dig into is dangerous. You need to be aware of that. I didn't kill Carter—"

"No kidding. Of course I know that! I can't believe you even felt the need to defend yourself."

He couldn't tell her how good it felt to have someone who wasn't family actually believe him, to not have to try to convince her that he wasn't a murdering traitor. Because the truth was, he had reached out to a few former contacts and they'd all told him to lose their number. "Look...Vitaly killed Carter. I saw him do it."

Lizzy swore softly.

He bit back the grief that still welled up inside him whenever he said Carter's name or thought about him. Considering he'd had a lot of time to himself the last few months, that had been often. "I've been working blind, basically, trying to dig for information on my own. But it's difficult to do that when I'm trying to stay alive and on the run." And while he was good with computers, he wasn't a hacker like Lizzy. He'd emailed himself that video of Vitaly killing Carter, but Kyle Bird had gotten to his account first and erased everything. If Ellis ever got his hands on his former boss, he didn't know that he'd be able to control his rage. "I don't even know if my former team knows about my relationship with you, but in case—"

"They do. They questioned me months ago," she said. "Hey, I actually helped your brother-in-law and sister out with something not too long ago. And your brother, but that was for something different. Freaking Bishops are racking up the favors lately," she murmured, her voice teasing.

Yeah he'd heard about that. His sister Evie and Lizzy had never actually met, as far as he knew, because they were different ages and Evie had split town as soon as she'd gotten recruited by the CIA. But Evie's husband knew Lizzy. "I need you to look into some other things related to the daughter. I found some bank accounts, including a big one in the Cayman Islands in her name. Millions of dollars' worth. I'm ninety-nine percent certain the accounts are real. I need to know if she's dirty, because until this morning I thought she was, but now…I'm questioning myself. And I don't know how to say this, but there are some dirty people in the DEA." He gave her Bird's name, the name of the CI who'd given up information on Arianna, and other pertinent info because Lizzy needed to know what she was working with. He didn't work for the DEA anymore and was wanted for murder so screw it. He was spilling secrets.

She snorted softly. "I don't know your former boss, but I'm not surprised by the revelation. Working for the DEA is too damn dangerous."

Yeah, he hated to admit it was true, but they'd had to get rid of a few bad apples in the last couple years—and that wasn't out of the norm. Of all the agencies, the DEA had the highest level of turnover and people who turned traitor. Not like he had stats or anything, but it made sense, considering the type of work they did. It was difficult to stay in the job long term because it was easy to lose focus on what they were trying to do. Especially for some people who were surrounded by criminals with ridiculous amounts of wealth and seemingly never got burned for it. It made it easier for certain agents to start thinking they should get a cut too. Ellis had grown up with wealth, so turning traitor for money had never occurred to him.

"Is there anyone you trust there?"

"Yeah...two people." He knew there were more trustworthy people in the administration but only two he'd stick his neck out for, and who he was certain would do the same for him. "But I'm not reaching out to them." He'd had to cut ties completely, had to make it easier on his friends because if they got targeted by the higher-ups due to their relationship with him, he'd never forgive himself. As far as he knew, both of them still had their jobs, but he knew they would've been questioned thoroughly after he got burned. And he knew they'd been watched heavily at least for the first month he was on the run.

"Names."

Sighing, he said, "Laura Leonard and Neil Vale. But leave them alone."

"I'm not contacting them. Just trying to get a picture of who you trust and who you don't. It might come in handy later if we need them."

Yeah, he understood that. "When you look into the woman, you've got to be careful because I don't know who else might be keeping tabs on her. No one can know of your interest in Arianna."

"This isn't my first rodeo, Ellis. Now how are you? Do you need anything? Money, a place to stay? I won't ask you where you are, but...let me help you if you need it."

He smiled at her concern, glad he hadn't been wrong about contacting her. Not that he'd thought he would be. He just hated bringing Lizzy into this. She was a mom now and he hadn't been joking about her husband. Porter would put a bullet in him if he thought Ellis had put her in danger. "You could probably find me if you tried." Because she was that good.

"I did try early on, but you were moving around too much. Since it was clear you didn't want to be found, I let it alone."

He sighed as he heard the water shut off and then the rustling of the shower curtain. "I'm close enough," he said quietly. "And I need this information whenever you get it. You've got that email address." When he'd contacted her earlier, he'd included a throwaway email address for her to send him any intel.

"Okay. Please stay safe."

"I will." After they disconnected, he took out the battery and broke the phone in half just as the bathroom door opened up.

Little waves of steam billowed out as Arianna stepped out of the bathroom wearing jeans and a red and white sweater with little dancing reindeer all over it. Jesus, she looked so young and innocent and that sinking feeling from last night was getting worse and worse. She looked everything like he thought an elementary school teacher should be, not a mastermind criminal who had millions of dollars offshore and was helping her stepfather flood the streets with poison.

He stood as she took another step into the room. "Are you hungry?"

She wrapped her arms around herself and nodded.

"Come on, then." He would feed her and give her all the information he had, and hope that when he next contacted Lizzy she would have more information for him. He couldn't let Arianna go until he knew for sure she wasn't involved in any of this.

"You're not wearing a mask," she murmured as they headed for the stairs, her voice tight. Edgy.

"I'm not planning on killing you, if that's what you're worried about." She was silent in front of him, not responding one way or the other. Which...was fair. "I took off my mask because I wanted to create some sort of trust between us," Ellis said as they entered the kitchen.

She turned to look at him with an *are you kidding me* expression.

He didn't blame her. He'd destroyed any option of trust between them. Hell, he'd set it on fire, then salted the earth. Still, he was going to have to try to gain her trust a little at this point if she was truly innocent. "My name is Ellis Bishop. You probably saw me on the news months ago." And a few times since then, though the media's interest in his story had waned. They had much bigger things to deal with right now.

Frowning, she sat at the center island as he passed her a banana. He really didn't have much here but he would give her access to everything he did. "Bishop..." She peeled the banana then her gaze flew to his. "Oh my God, I didn't recognize you because of your beard. I know of your mom and sister-in-law," she rasped out. "You're that agent who murdered..." She trailed off, the last few words a whisper as she set down the banana, staring at him in horror.

"Eat. It's been a long time since you had any food in your system. And I didn't kill anyone. I'm being set up."

Frowning, she picked up the banana and started eating.

"I've got coffee or water," he said. Then he snorted. "Or beer." A six-pack he hadn't touched since he'd bought it weeks ago from a gas station with no security cameras.

Her eyes flared with anger then but she quickly masked it and he wasn't sure what he'd said.

"Water is fine." Her words were tight.

He grabbed her a bottle from the fridge and slid it across the countertop. "I've got more fruit and oatmeal. Or Pop-Tarts?"

"Oatmeal is fine."

"For the record, because I didn't know you knew my family, no one is aware that I kidnapped you."

"Is that supposed to make me feel better?"

"No, I just didn't want you to think my family..."

"Is as horrible as you?" she asked pointedly, taking the final bite of her banana, polishing it off neatly.

"More or less." When he heard a soft ding on his other burner phone indicating he had an email message, he checked it as he put the oatmeal in the microwave. He still kept an eye on Arianna out of the corner of his eye, and as he read over the details his gut tightened even more. He looked over the PDF documents, quickly scanning them, but Lizzy's message was the most important. *Looks like the daughter is clean. Accounts in her name were set up by someone else. It's a very tidy job, however. Professional. Someone wants to set her up for something. Maybe not now, but eventually. Looks as if they're laying groundwork. And I had to dig for this information. Government or a real pro did this. She might be in trouble. Gonna keep digging. Also, your former CI is dead. Killed in a drive-by.*

Frowning, he tucked his cell phone into his back pocket and looked across the countertop at Arianna with new eyes. He felt like the shittiest person in the world. He'd kidnapped an innocent woman from her home last night. Maybe he did deserve to go to jail after all. Once he cleared his name from killing Carter, he would come clean about kidnapping Arianna. "When you're done eating, I want to show you something."

She simply watched him instead of responding so he pulled the oatmeal out of the microwave.

"Are you going to eat?" she asked as he set the bowl in front of her.

He leaned against the countertop and shook his head. But he could tell he was unnerving her—no surprise, since he'd kidnapped her—so he started making coffee even though he didn't want any more. As soon as he started moving around, she dug into her food. "Are you sure you don't want more?"

"I'm kind of afraid I might throw it up if I think too long on…where I am."

Fair enough. He wanted to apologize to her, especially after reading Lizzy's email, but first he wanted to show her the boards he'd set up. He needed to gauge her reaction to that as well.

It didn't take long for her to finish eating. When she was done, he gave her another banana in case she decided she was still hungry, then motioned for her to follow him back upstairs.

She watched him warily but had no choice but to go where he directed.

"Second door on the left," he said behind her.

She stepped into the room he'd set up as an office, and before he'd taken one step in past her she'd lunged at the pistol he'd left on the desk.

Moving lightning fast, she whipped it around and held it at him with shaking hands. Her eyes were wild as she tried to point it straight at him.

"That's not loaded," he murmured.

And she looked as if she'd never held a weapon in her entire life, though he knew her stepfather had given her one, which lined up with the one he'd found at her place.

Her hands trembled even harder. "Put your hands up!"

He simply shut the door behind him and stepped forward. "Just put it down."

She stared at him, her pupils dilating, her breathing growing harsher. "I told you to put your hands up!"

"Look—"

Click.

He stared in surprise as she pulled the trigger.

He wasn't sure who was more surprised—her, or him that she'd actually pulled it.

"Oh my God," she rasped out, the pistol falling from her hand. "I..."

"Well I'm really glad it wasn't loaded now," he said dryly as he picked it up and tucked it into the back of his pants. "It's not loaded because I didn't want to risk you getting hurt."

"Are you freaking kidding me!" She was definitely coming out of her dazed state. "Wait...did you kidnap me with an empty gun?"

"Yes."

She turned away from him, slowly spinning in a circle as she muttered curses to herself. Suddenly she froze as she started taking in the rest of the room.

He'd set up two giant boards similar to the ones his team had at work. The technology he'd had before had been a lot better but this worked just as well for his purposes. He had most of the knowledge locked away in his brain anyway, but being able to look at everything in such a huge visual was helpful.

"What is all this?" She stared at everything, those pretty green eyes wide in a combination of horror and fascination.

"My investigation."

"Into...what? And why am I on it?" More indignation punctuated each word.

"Because until this morning I thought you were involved in dealing weapons and laundering money."

She walked up to the board without even glancing at him. "I recognize this guy," she said, tapping her finger against Carter's picture. "I remember because he was so good-looking. This is the guy you—"

"I didn't kill him," he snapped out. "He was my partner and best friend. Your stepfather killed him."

Arianna spun to face him, her eyes flaring with anger. "Oh yeah, sure."

"Your stepfather works for some very dirty people— and is just plain dirty. And I *saw* him kill Carter with my own eyes. Carter was my best friend! I was godfather to his kids. I'm sure I'm not anymore but...I loved him like a brother. I never could have hurt him, ever. And if I'd just gotten there a few minutes earlier, I could have saved him. Instead, Vitaly shot him point-blank and didn't bat an eye."

If he'd just been a few minutes earlier. He'd replayed that day over and over in his mind, especially at night when he was trying to sleep. It was like an awful scene that was set on repeat.

He gritted his teeth, forcing himself to lock down any emotions that tried to bubble up. He couldn't release the reins now, not when he needed to convince her that he was telling the truth. When he'd kidnapped her, he'd erased any olive branch of trust that might have grown between them. Even so, he was going to try and see if he could still use her. Well, not *use* her exactly, but he wanted to see if there was any hope that she might help him.

Because yeah, he was so desperate that he was hoping a civilian who clearly had no weapons training could help him. At least what he needed her for had nothing to do with weapons.

She paused, watching him carefully, and he wasn't sure what she saw.

This was a lost cause. He just needed to let her go and figure this shit out on his own. Now that he had Lizzy on board he should be able to get more done anyway.

CHAPTER FIVE

Arianna watched her kidnapper, a man she actually recognized from the news. He was insanely handsome, something she hated that she noticed now that the mask was off.

It was strange—he had a rugged quality and looked nothing like his mug shots, nothing like the images the news had flashed on the television feeds. In those he'd looked scary and as if he hadn't had a shower in days. Now? Yeah, he was kinda scary but also very, very handsome. Even with the beard that he could probably stand to trim a little. Heck, it kinda gave him an even edgier, sexier look. His hair was a little long too, as if he hadn't had time to cut it—which he probably hadn't since he was busy hiding from law enforcement.

"So you didn't kill your partner?" she asked carefully, watching him. She'd been going to AA meetings for three years and she was very good at weeding out the liars, the people who couldn't admit they had a problem and wanted to blame others for every single bad thing in their life. Because if they didn't take responsibility, then nothing was their fault. Certainly made drinking yourself into oblivion a lot easier.

She'd been one of those people once upon a time and they were easy for her to spot. But that was the thing with recovering alcoholics. Once you admitted you had a problem, you started telling the truth about everything. It was a cathartic type of thing. At least it was for her. Like with smokers who finally quit, and were always trying to get others to quit as well.

She wasn't sure if Bishop had killed his partner or not, but the grief in his eyes when he'd talked about his dead friend was so very real she felt it like a punch to the gut. She remembered the images of the dead man—he'd had a California surfer-type look to him and the media had gone crazy splashing his image and ones of his picture-perfect family everywhere.

"I don't care if you believe me. Okay...I *do* care if you believe me, but I didn't kill Carter. I'd have taken a bullet for him. Vitaly pulled the trigger. I was there."

There was something more he wanted to say, she was sure of it, but he tightened his jaw and looked back at the boards.

"Like I told you last night, the bank accounts in your name are real. And I've come across some new information this morning that indicates the person who tipped me off you were involved is dead. Which is a mighty big coincidence. I'll show you everything I have. Someone is setting you up for something. Though I'm not sure what." His frown deepened.

She didn't understand any of this. Who would target her? Maybe her stepfather, but...why would he? They might not have a loving, close relationship, but there was no animosity between them. There was *nothing* between them. Just polite civility when they saw each other. And he even checked in with her during the week.

"Do you recognize any of these men?" He indicated the boards, which included little clusters of pictures. Many of them included her stepfather, but there were a couple sections with pictures that simply had question marks above them. There was also a section on her with another question mark. Some pictures had been taken of her leaving school or her house. *Wow.* Okay, she was just going to move past that for now.

"I've seen two of them in passing." She pointed at two men. "At my stepfather's estate in Orlando. Who are the rest of these people?" She looked at every image, curious—and horrified—by all of it.

A pause. "Your stepfather's associates, mainly." Another pause. "And some DEA agents I suspect of being dirty. But mainly known criminals, though not all have records. They're mostly mid-level assholes who run drugs and weapons."

She scanned the images again, digesting his words. "What about this guy?" She indicated a grainy sepia-colored image of her stepfather with a man who looked slightly familiar.

To her surprise, Bishop pulled out his phone and pulled up a search engine. Then he handed her the phone.

Tentatively, she took it. "What's this for?"

"Search for Benigno Saltillo."

She typed in the name and stared at a few news articles listing the man from the picture as a drug runner from Central America. He was now dead. She looked back at the picture of her stepfather with the guy. "This doesn't mean anything," she murmured, but couldn't put any heat behind it as a lead weight settled in her gut. Because it did mean something.

He took the phone from her then swiped his finger across the screen a few times.

She watched as various documents popped up.

"Just swipe right. I can get you hard copies later, but I just received these documents."

She looked at the different bank accounts in her name as well as the accompanying documents. There was a big one in Grand Cayman, but a couple other small ones in Europe. They'd all been opened up very recently.

Feeling sick, she looked around again before basically collapsing on the small cot with rumpled sheets in the corner of the room. She vaguely wondered if he'd been sleeping here while she'd been cuffed to the headboard in the other room. "So...I don't know what to do with all this. But I want to know what you want from me." She tossed the phone next to her, not bothering to try and dial 911. He probably had the damn phone blocked. A tension headache spread across the back of her skull as she tried to digest all this information. Maybe it was lies, but if it wasn't... What was going on? And why lie about this anyway?

"I want the same thing I wanted before. I want you to empty out those bank accounts." There was a sort of desperation in his eyes.

She swallowed hard. "Then what?"

"Then I'm going to use that money to draw your stepfather out into the open. He's been siphoning that money away without his boss's knowledge for something. And he's going to want it back." His eyes darkened with rage as he talked about Vitaly.

"What if I won't help you? What will you do to me?" She couldn't help the tremor in her voice. She was pretty sure her stepfather was into some bad stuff, but that didn't mean Ellis was someone she could trust. The man had kidnapped her and was holding her hostage. *Trust? Ha.*

He took a step toward her, his huge body vibrating with...something, and for a moment pure terror punched through her, but then he turned away from her. His massive shoulders were bunched up tight. "Nothing. I'm not going to do anything to you. I'm not going to hurt you. And even if you were just like your stepfather, I...couldn't hurt you either." There was a note of self-loathing in his voice as he made the statement, as if he was annoyed at himself.

"Let me go, then," she whispered, too scared to believe he might actually do it. "Please take me home." She needed to get away from here, to get away from him.

To her surprise he nodded, though all his muscles were pulled taut. "Fine. Grab your bag. I'll have to put the hood over your face for the drive back."

Her heart was an erratic tattoo in her chest. She so desperately wanted to believe he was actually going to take her home. He seemed so earnest and kind of defeated right now. And his stupid gun had been empty. But maybe that was all a ploy to... To what? What if those accounts were *real?*

She swallowed hard as dozens upon dozens of questions ran through her mind. She couldn't wrap her head around any of it. She needed to go to someone in law enforcement, needed to talk to somebody about what was going on, especially if random bank accounts had been opened in her name.

As she grabbed her bag, she knew she also needed to acknowledge that the thought of her stepfather killing someone somehow didn't surprise her. For reasons she did *not* want to think about right now.

God, how was she going to face him or even talk to him now? Even if she wanted to go back to her life and pretend everything was normal, she couldn't.

Everything had changed, and she had no idea what she was going to do about it.

CHAPTER SIX

At the sound of a garage door opening and the SUV shutting off, Arianna tensed. But when Ellis opened the door and took her hood off, she realized they were in her garage. He really had brought her home. And he hadn't tied her up this time—though he had made her lie in the back on the floor again.

"I've got your phone but I took the battery out last night before we left. I'm going to dump the pieces at a park about half a mile from here."

She stared at him as they stepped into the laundry room. "Why?"

"So it'll take you time to reach your phone and call your stepfather. Or the police."

"Are you for real?"

"Yes. I don't think he'll be able to figure out where I took you, but I'm getting a head start. Also, you need to put a lock on your security system app."

"Are you seriously giving me advice?" she asked as he shut the door behind them. She was glad to be back home even if it was with him. And even if she was still scared.

"I was able to get into your house relatively easily. Also…I recommend the police over your stepfather. They're already looking for me anyway, and this way you'll have some sort of protection. Someone set those accounts up and my money is on Vitaly. He might just decide it's easier to eliminate you as a problem if you tell him about the accounts."

She stared at him, confusion swirling inside her, but then she sighed. It was hard to digest that her stepfather could ever want to kill her. But she'd had time to think in the back of the SUV on the way here, and while nothing was clear—at all—she couldn't think of one good reason why Ellis was still in the country, or even the state at least. It didn't make any sense. If he was guilty, he should be starting over somewhere. "Come inside with me—unless you want to hang out in my laundry room?" Where she still had some delicate panties hanging up, she realized. Ignoring them, she raised an eyebrow at him, waiting for his answer.

He frowned at her.

"If you're guilty of killing your friend, you're going to a whole lot of trouble to stay in the country trying to solve a crime you allegedly committed."

He followed her into the kitchen, his expression carefully neutral as he shut the door behind him. "Are you saying you believe me?"

"I'm saying I don't *not* believe you. All those pictures, all that evidence on your boards, it's a lot to take in. And the bank accounts... Not to mention you could easily have tried to get a ransom for me or just killed me or done a hundred other awful things."

His gun hadn't even been loaded when he took her. And he was so damn earnest, the truth practically rolled off him in waves. She was going with her gut right now. Even if she might regret this later.

"Say we go down to the Cayman Islands. How would I even empty out these alleged accounts?" She wanted to see with her own eyes that they were real, to find out if she had access to them. And if they were real, then...her stepfather was very likely guilty of everything else he'd said. As she sat at the island in her kitchen, she felt oddly out of place. Nothing felt real anymore. It was like the last twelve hours had changed everything and now she was drifting. Not to mention his presence in her home was unsettling.

Ellis leaned against the countertop opposite her, his big arms crossed over his chest. "I don't know that I want you to empty them out anymore."

She stared at him. "I thought that was the whole reason you kidnapped me."

"That was when I thought you were dirty. I thought I'd be able to use you against your stepfather. Now...I'm thinking of a better way to handle things. I don't want you involved anymore. That might mean you have to go into protective custody once you talk to the Feds or police about those accounts, but—"

"Okay, stop right there. That's insane. I haven't seen or done anything. I'm not going into some crazy witness protection program. I don't even have anything to offer them so why would the cops help me?"

"Whoever set those accounts up is trying to frame you for something. Or they're using your name to funnel money so no blowback comes on to them. It might not be about a frame-up. I'm not sure yet, but I'm going to figure that part out too."

"So we take away their power and take away all their money." Someone was using her freaking name to funnel dirty money? Yeah, screw them. And if it was her stepfather? *Ugh.* Bishop said he'd seen Vitaly kill his friend. What if...it was true?

"You could go to the police."

She snorted. She didn't trust the cops to do anything right. Not state level anyway. Maybe the Feds would be better, but she resisted the urge to sneer at the thought of local cops handling anything. In her experience they were useless.

He frowned slightly, his brow furrowing. "You don't like cops?"

"They botched two cases I was directly involved in." So no, not a fan.

His expression sobered. "I know the locals in Orlando handled your brother's...death."

She nodded tightly. "Yeah. Obviously you know that my brother died of an overdose since you've looked into my family. He was actually my half-brother but I never thought of him like that. He was just my Max, my baby brother. I loved him. And when he died, the cops treated the whole case like garbage. They wouldn't even entertain the thought that maybe it hadn't been an overdose. To them he was just a loser junkie who'd gotten what he deserved."

They'd also completely dropped the ball in her rape case, made her feel as if she deserved what had happened.

The on-scene officer who'd originally talked to her had asked stupid, offensive questions. But she shoved that thought down. She was not opening up that can of worms right now. Not with this stranger.

When her doorbell suddenly rang, they both froze, but he moved into action first, a smooth and lethal predator. "Are you expecting anyone?" He stepped around the countertop as if to go answer her door.

"No, but do you really think it's a good idea for you to answer my door, a wanted felon?"

He froze and she could see him fighting the urge to take charge.

"I'm answering the door. You're either here when I get back or you're not." She knew there was a good chance he might run. Maybe that would be easier in the long run, though she still had no idea what to do about the knowledge of those bank accounts.

Instead of waiting for a response she turned away, because she wasn't sure if she wanted him to stay or not. Yes, she wanted answers but he was on the run for his life. Wasn't like he was doing so well for himself. Maybe she'd be better off reaching out to...someone. She wouldn't talk to the local cops, but one of the guys at AA had a brother who was a Fed.

When she looked through the peephole of her front door, she froze for a moment. *What the heck?* Opening the door, she stared in surprise at her stepfather's assistant, Zach Foster. Though after seeing the pictures and short anecdotes on Ellis's whiteboards, she didn't think Zach was an assistant at all. More like a hired criminal, from all accounts. Even if he didn't look like what she thought a criminal would. And yeah, she knew that was stereotyping but he wasn't covered in tattoos, his blond hair was cut military short and he had an easy, affable smile that made him seem approachable. He even wore khakis and a polo shirt.

"Is everything okay? Is it my stepfather?"

He nodded. "Your stepfather called you multiple times yesterday. And texted you. You didn't respond and he got worried. Since I was in Miami, I told him I'd stop by to check on you."

Okay, this was beyond weird. She raised an eyebrow, not bothering to hide her confusion or annoyance. "I'm fine, as you can see."

"Did you just get in?" he asked, making her frown again.

"Excuse me? Why?" A little tingle started at the base of her skull. Something weird—well, weirder—was going on. Why would he even ask that? Had he been watching her house or something?

He lifted a shoulder. "Your stepfather is just worried about you."

The truth of that statement wasn't reflected in his eyes.

So she sighed, wanting to deflect any more questions at this point. "Look, I'm dating someone new. I stayed over at his place last night and I turned off my phone."

The tension in his shoulders eased. "You have a new boyfriend?"

"I wouldn't call him that. I *just* started dating him. He's a teacher too. It's very new so I didn't want to mention anything to Vitaly."

He nodded and took a small step backward, now half-smiling in understanding. "Just make sure you text your father so he knows you're okay. I told him it was no big deal, but you know how he worries."

She wasn't so sure it was worry, but more of a need for him to control everything. He'd been like that with her mother too, but her mom hadn't cared so Arianna hadn't either. Now...she wondered if he really was into money laundering and drug running—and murder. Bishop had her questioning everything, and the truth was, she'd always suspected that Vitaly had been capable of...

She cleared her throat. "I will," she said, though she had no doubt that Zach was going to call Vitaly immediately anyway. She also wanted to tell him not to stop by her house without calling but it would be rude and she just wanted him gone. They talked only a few more moments before she made a quick escape and shut the door behind him.

As she stepped back into her kitchen, she saw that Ellis was gone. She stopped and listened but didn't hear him moving around anywhere. Shoving out a sigh, she stepped toward the island. She wasn't sure how she felt about him being gone—or what she was going to do with her new knowledge.

"Is it normal for him to stop by your house unannounced?" Ellis's deep voice sounded right behind her, making her bite back a scream.

But she couldn't stop from jumping in shock as she turned to face him. "I thought you left."

"Still here. So?"

Her heart was still racing but she shook her head. "No, it's not normal. It's very, *very* out of the ordinary. It's not like he lives in the city and I don't buy that he just happened to be in Miami. I actually didn't realize he knew where I lived, to be honest." So today was just getting more and more concerning.

"If I had to guess, your stepfather has some sort of tracking software on your phone, and when you turned it off—well, when I turned it off and took the battery out—he wasn't able to track you. Foster is his second in charge. It matters that he sent *him* and not some other jackass."

She stared at him as he so casually mentioned tracking software. "There's no way…" She trailed off, realizing that right about now she couldn't afford to just ignore this. "How can I tell if he's got tracking software on my phone?"

He pulled out her cell phone and put the battery back in, then turned it on. He held it out for her thumbprint, then, holding it out for her to see, he pulled up the settings and went into some random files and found what was definitely tracking software.

"I should have checked for this before," he muttered to himself in disgust.

She stared at it in horror. "Oh my God!" She grabbed for her phone, ready to uninstall and delete it, but he shook his head.

"If you get rid of it, he'll know you've done it. Better to leave it."

Swallowing hard, she shoved her phone away, not wanting to touch the thing. The tension headache was back, spreading around the back of her skull. It would be so damn easy to have a drink right now, to just ignore what was going on. But the urge to drink wasn't there, for now at least.

Because it wouldn't help her. No, it would only make things worse. Right now she needed answers and going down the rabbit hole again would only create a new set of problems. "Okay, let's do this," she said crossing her arms over her chest.

He blinked at her. "Do what, exactly?"

"I want to see the account in the Caymans." From the paperwork she'd looked at, the bank was in Grand Cayman. "I want to go down there and see if all this is true. And if it is…I'm going to close the account." She wasn't sure what her next move would be, but if her stepfather thought he could somehow use her name to launder money for him, use her for whatever? *Hell no.* For now she wasn't going to think about if he would actually hurt her. Vitaly had loved her mother, had been heartbroken when she'd died of breast cancer, but…Arianna wasn't so sure that would stop him from hurting Arianna if she crossed him.

Ellis's blue eyes darkened slightly "Are you serious?"

"What else am I going to do right now? It's pretty clear that someone is trying to set me up for something, though I'm not sure what. Your own people have set *you* up."

He looked stunned. "You believe me?"

"Should I not?"

"I just don't know if heading down to the Caymans is a good idea."

Was he kidding her right now? "What, now that I'm a willing participant and not a hostage, my coming along has lost its appeal?"

He blinked in surprise. "You're kind of a smartass."

"I'm aware. It's a defect of mine."

"I wouldn't call it that." The barest hint of a smile pulled at his lips. Or she thought it might be one. It was impossible to tell since she didn't really know him.

"Why are you fighting me on this?"

"I don't like involving you in this anymore." He sat down at the center island, looking almost sullen.

"Then what are we going to do? I don't even know who to turn to at this point. If my stepfather killed your friend, he needs to pay for his crimes. And why is someone setting up random accounts in my name? None of this is good!" And the only way she could really know if the accounts were real was to go to the bank herself. Afterward she'd have to figure out if her stepfather was behind opening them—and what to do about that. She had no clue who would have jurisdiction over money laundering either. The FBI maybe?

"You don't seem to be having a hard time believing he's capable of murder." There was an odd note in his tone.

"If I'm being honest, I've always suspected his businesses might not be on the up-and-up. But I never suspected drugs or guns! Never in a million years. I just thought he was sort of maybe a middleman who bought and sold art and antiques and stuff like that. He has way too many security guys around his Orlando estate and he's always got random pieces of fine art popping up in his office or his home. And now to find out he or someone close to him potentially set up a bank account in my name? Screw that." She tempered her anger and forced herself to think clearly, to go over her options. Not that she was even sure what they were at this point.

"We can find someone in law enforcement for you to talk to—"

"And then what? Someone seizes those accounts? Who's to say I won't go to jail for some kind of crazy fraud or something? I'm not going to trust some random cops with the rest of my life. No, I'm going to help you. You seem to understand what's going on here better than anyone. And I'm going to help myself. I'm not going to jail for something I didn't do."

He scrubbed a hand over his face, looking exhausted.

"How much sleep did you get last night?" she asked suddenly. He looked as if he might fall over at any moment.

He frowned at her. "Like three hours. Once you were out, I biked back to the church and grabbed my SUV."

So that explained how he'd gotten the SUV, because he'd kidnapped her in her car originally. "Biked?"

"I took your bicycle from your house before we went to my safe house—I put it in your trunk in case I needed it."

The image of him riding around on her teal and yellow beach cruiser was absurd and she found herself fighting a laugh because it would have come out manic and crazed-sounding.

She rubbed a hand over her face. Her gut instinct was telling her that he was being honest with her about everything. He'd been on the run and in hiding for months trying to clear his name. She couldn't even imagine what kind of existence that was, the kind of toll it would take on someone. "So are we going to do this or not?"

There was a long pause as he watched her. His thick arms were crossed over his chest, his pale eyes intense. Finally he sighed, shoving a hand through his dark, slightly unruly hair. "I can get us out of the country. You'll need to bring your passport and another ID for the bank, but we won't be traveling through standard channels. We'll be entering another country illegally, so think about whether or not you want to do that."

Yeah, like that was the worst of her problems right now. "Okay. How are we going to get to the Caymans?"

"First we're going to get out of here by boat—a yacht. Then we'll take a private plane once we're out of the States. Coming back we'll likely just fly straight to Miami, but that could change depending on anything that happens down in Grand Cayman."

"What are the chances of us getting caught?" She figured small, considering he was trying to stay off the radar of anyone in law enforcement.

"Very small, but shit happens. That said, if anything does happen and we get caught, I'll just take the fall for kidnapping you. You won't get in trouble for anything."

"I can deal with that."

He watched her carefully, as if trying to read her mind. "We're also going to have to trash your house a little bit. Make it look as if I took you by force, because I'm betting your stepfather will come here once we do this. We're going to have to leave your cell phone behind."

That all made sense. "I can mess up my house effectively if you tell me what it needs to look like."

He gave her the side-eye. "You're handling all of this remarkably well."

She snorted. "I'm glad I'm convincing, because I'm not handling this well. I'm freaking out right now. So let's do this before I change my mind."

CHAPTER SEVEN

"Thank you for doing this," Ellis said to his sister Evie as he stepped out into the main cabin of Dylan's yacht. Arianna was getting settled into the master stateroom where they would be hiding out for the next couple hours.

Evie's jet-black hair was pulled back into a high ponytail on her head, her makeup was an overdone "glam" look and she wore a weird-looking bathing suit she said was "trendy" as part of her own cover today. She and Dylan, her billionaire husband, were taking his yacht out for the next few days and Evie was posing as his pretty socialite wife who wanted a quick getaway.

In reality, she was a former CIA agent and Ellis was damn glad to have her on his side. Because of her, he was able to easily get out of the country.

"You don't ever have to thank me for this. I'm just glad you finally reached out. I rarely say this, but today should go off without a hitch. This crew loves Dylan and won't ask any questions."

Arm wrapped tightly around Evie's shoulders, Dylan nodded. "We've got this."

Ellis still couldn't believe his little sister was married—or that he'd missed the wedding. He was just glad she'd found someone she loved, and who would do anything for her. The man was sticking his neck out for Ellis as well and he didn't have to. If anything, Ellis would have understood if he'd said no. "Well thank you anyway. Both of you. You're taking a risk," he said, looking at Dylan.

Of course the other man just brushed it off.

Evie grinned suddenly, reminding Ellis of the mischievous teenager she'd once been. "Evan's going to be so pissed when he finds out he wasn't asked to help out with this."

"You sure as shit aren't going to tell him," he growled. He didn't even like bringing Evie into this. He didn't want more people he cared about getting involved.

"We'll see." She glanced over her shoulder toward the back of the big yacht, as if she could see past the doors and hallway to the master stateroom. "How is she settling in?"

Arianna. "Good, I think. I still don't understand why she's doing this." And part of that was giving him pause. She was certainly making everything so much easier for him right now. But she'd jumped into all of this headfirst.

"I get it," Evie said. "Deep down she probably doesn't believe the accounts are real. She's probably thinking that once she gets there, she'll discover it's all a big mistake and that this was a misunderstanding. Or she's just pissed and wants to fight back at whoever is trying to tie her to fraud or money laundering. I'd be pissed if someone did that to me and you better believe I'd make them pay."

He snorted because his sister was more likely to just shoot someone who tried to mess with her. But maybe she was right. Arianna had admitted that part of her had always suspected her stepfather was into less than savory dealings. Ellis had a feeling that was a big part of her decision to do this.

And she didn't seem to trust cops. She'd told him why she didn't, but he had a feeling that there was more to it and he wanted to know everything. He'd dug into her background and he hadn't found anything that should warrant such a mistrust of law enforcement. Yeah, the way her brother's death was handled mattered but...his gut was telling him there was more.

"I'm going to head back there," he said, wanting to see how Arianna was doing.

"You know what to do if you hear a knock on the door," Dylan said, glancing over his shoulder toward the main doors. "Now get out of here. I don't want any of the staff to see you."

He nodded and clasped hands with Dylan before pulling his sister into a tight hug.

He must have taken her off guard because she let out a little squeak before squeezing him back just as tight.

Ellis turned and headed toward the glass and wood doorway to the hallway. He and Arianna were staying out of sight and the crew had strict instructions not to go into the master stateroom. It was kind of a weird request, but considering Dylan owned this yacht and he was Midas rich, no one was going to question his eccentricities.

Ellis quietly slipped into the stateroom and locked the door behind him. The room was huge, with heavy dark wood paneling but bright white and blue bedding that seemed to brighten up the place. There was a sitting area with two cream-colored tufted chairs, a table with a tray of food and a huge flat-screen TV over an electric fireplace. There was also a little desk area and a fairly large closet. All in rich wood tones. With the big bay of tinted windows, however, it didn't feel as small as it should, given all the wood. Even so, he was very aware of being in this space with just the two of them for the next couple hours.

"Everything okay?" Arianna sat on the bed in dark jeans and a green T-shirt, her knees pulled up to her chest. A navy blue throw blanket was rumpled next to her.

He nodded as he glanced at the spread of food that had been in here when they'd first arrived. "Yeah. We're good to go. Should be setting sail in the next ten to twenty minutes."

"Good." Stretching her legs out, she moved the mostly empty plate of food she'd grabbed earlier to the side. Her feet twitched back and forth every few moments, her actions jerky.

He stepped farther into the room and made a small plate of food for himself. "Having second thoughts?"

"Well, yeah. I mean I'm doing this, but…I'm still nervous. This feels surreal. I feel like someone else has taken over my body and my life."

"Welcome to the club," he said half laughingly, though there was no humor in his voice as he went to join her on the huge bed. He sat on the opposite side, giving her plenty of room. "Trust me, I never envisioned this being my life either."

She grabbed a little square of cheese and popped it into her mouth. Her feet still twitched back and forth in a fast rhythm.

"We can turn around now. We can stop this whole thing if you change your mind." It was clear she was keyed up and he didn't want to pressure her into anything. After this, there was no turning back.

"Jeez, I haven't changed my mind. I'm just a ball of nervous energy, that's all. Cut me some slack."

He shoved out a sigh and smiled at her tone. "All right." He glanced over at the drinks the staff had provided. "You didn't want anything to drink?"

She gave him a dark, searching look. "I'm an alcoholic."

He blinked, his eyes widening. "What?"

"You kidnapped me outside an AA meeting... Still, I find it hard to believe you're that much of a dick to keep mentioning alcohol. So cut it out."

Uh, what? "I thought you attended those grief meetings at the church. I never... Shit, I'm sorry." He was sorry for a lot lately. "No wonder you looked like you wanted to throat punch me when I offered you a beer at the house."

She watched him carefully. "So you really aren't being a dick?"

"No. I really didn't know. I never went into the church, and since you lost your mom and brother so close together, I just assumed..." He scrubbed a hand over his face. "You're barely twenty-five."

She lifted a shoulder. "Yep. And I'm lucky enough to have figured out my problem early in life." There was a whole lot of sarcasm lacing her words.

"I didn't mean... Okay I did mean it. You're pretty young."

"Trust me. It doesn't matter. I've been in AA and completely sober for three years. Technically I've been in AA three and a half years but it didn't stick until after six months of meetings. I haven't had a drop of alcohol in almost three years exactly. One thousand ninety-three days, if you want me to get specific."

He blinked. "Damn. I'm sorry."

She lifted a shoulder. "Thank you. I take it one day at a time. And I know I was being a smartass before but I'm lucky compared to a lot of people. I didn't lose a lot of friends because of it, mainly because all my friends were partying hard years ago. Some still do. And I did cut those people out of my life just for my own sanity. After I started going to AA, and hearing all of the horror stories, some so much worse than mine, I thought maybe I really didn't have a problem. That I could handle drinking in small quantities. So I experimented, tried to have a glass of wine here or there. But it was *never* small quantities for me. Once I start, I can't stop. It's a compulsion and I give in to it every time. I hate myself the next day, but it doesn't change anything. That's when I knew I had a real problem and if I didn't treat it, I was going to end up killing myself. Or in jail. Or hurting someone else. Maybe in jail for hurting someone."

"I don't even know what to say." It was brave of her to be so honest about it.

She gave him a ghost of a smile. "That's okay. Most people don't. Though to be fair, I don't tell most people that I'm a recovering alcoholic when first meeting them. Or even at all. Some of my friends have no idea. They think I just don't like to drink. But you did kidnap me, so I feel like we are on a completely different wavelength than most people."

He let out an unexpected laugh at her blunt words and dry tone. It really was no wonder she was handling things so damn well. She had a sense of humor, and he found himself wishing he'd met her under very different circumstances. But he shoved that thought down *hard*. There was no room for that here.

"So," he said as the engine rumbled to life below them. Yep, they would be getting out of here soon. "Is the reason you're doing this because you think those bank accounts aren't real?" He didn't want to tell her that had been his sister's thought, because he hadn't told Arianna who was helping them. Ellis had just told her that his friend was letting them use his yacht. He didn't think she was lying to him, but he still wasn't telling her about his sister's involvement. If Arianna didn't know about them, she couldn't tell anyone. Plausible deniability.

She paused but finally nodded. "Part of me hopes this is all a big mistake, that you're totally wrong. That we'll get to the bank and they'll have no idea who I am."

He nodded, not surprised. Then he cleared his throat. "Look...I'm sorry for the way I took you."

"The gun wasn't loaded," she said offhandedly, but he saw the spark of raw pain in her eyes.

"Yeah, but you didn't know that. I had to have terrified you and...I'm ashamed of all of it. I researched you but I should have dug deeper. Clearly. I shouldn't have made such a huge mistake. You didn't deserve what I did and...I'm just sorry. If I could go back in time, I would. I swear I'll help you figure out who set up those accounts. And if it's the last thing I do, I'll make sure you're cleared of any wrongdoing, should it ever come to that." Though he was going to make damn sure it didn't. He was going to figure out who had set up those accounts and why. "And if...you end up having nightmares because of what I did and need counseling or something, I'll pay for it."

Her eyes were wide as she stared at him. "Um...okay. Thank you. And apology accepted. What you did was messed up—like, beyond—but stop beating yourself up."

"Seriously?"

"No. You can keep beating yourself up for a while." She grinned. "At least until after we figure out what's going on with these accounts. Then once you clear your name, you're totally going to make it up to me."

He leaned back against the bed as he faced her. She really was beautiful and only now was it hitting him full force. Before, when he'd thought she was a criminal, it had been easy to dismiss her beauty. Beauty in general was easy to ignore. But she was...funny and smart. And holding up like a champ. And that was sexy more than her looks. "How?"

"Oh, I'll think of something. This yacht for instance?"

Ellis blinked, staring at the stunning woman. Her dark hair was down around her face in soft waves, she had no makeup on, and there was a slightly mischievous twitch to her full lips. Lips he wanted to stare at, but resisted the urge. "You want a yacht?"

"Uh, no. Can you imagine the maintenance?" Her grin widened and it hit him right in the solar plexus how stunning she was when she smiled like that. "But I do want to throw a big party on it. Or take it out for a day and go diving. And I don't want to be stuck in a room, hiding from the staff. I want to enjoy every single perk this thing has to offer."

He watched her for a long moment, entranced by everything about her. "I think I can manage that."

"Good. It'll give me something to look forward to after..." She leaned back against the pillows, her smile fading. "After all this. I don't even know what I'm going to do if those accounts are real."

They'd talked about what the next steps would be after this, but he knew what she meant. "One step at a time."

She snorted softly. "Yeah, I tell myself that every single day."

"What's it like teaching third grade?" he asked after a pause. He'd been watching her—stalking her really—but he hadn't paid attention to any of the small things. He'd been more concerned with getting her schedule right, with making sure he knew exactly when to take her. *Ugh.* Thinking of that brought up another wave of guilt he was certain he'd be living with for a long time.

"Fun. Challenging. Exhausting. And fun," she said again. "Kids are so great at that age. So ready to learn, eager to help out, and they're just nice. Sure, they can pick on each other, but at eight and nine they're still learning about the world around them and they're so full of curiosity. If they hurt someone's feelings, it's never malicious. And they apologize and mean it." Her eyes practically shone as she talked about teaching and her kids.

"Sounds like they're lucky to have you."

"I'm lucky to be able to do what I love. Because it's sure not about the money," she added on a laugh.

"So…you want kids of your own?" He was asking a lot of personal questions but they had a lot of time to kill. And he wanted to know everything about her. The real Arianna. The one who wasn't anything like he'd first assumed.

"Wow, a kidnapper and super nosy," she said, smiling as she reached for another piece of cheese. "Maybe. I love all my kids but it's also *really* nice coming home to a quiet house at the end of the day."

He narrowed his gaze at the hitch in her tone. "What?"

"You're holding back."

"Of course I am." She sighed. "Fine. I'm afraid to have kids because of my alcoholism. For so many reasons tied to that."

Ah. "Yeah, I can understand that." He knew some men, and women, who drank far too much but they were all undercover agents. He understood what had driven them to drink. Arianna was so damn young and he wondered if something had triggered her drinking or if it was just genetic.

"I also haven't dated in...forever. And I have no plans or prospects on the horizon either."

He couldn't understand why someone hadn't scooped her up. Seriously, she was funny and gorgeous. Men in Miami were stupid.

"So what about you?" she continued. "Turnabout is fair play and you've literally held me at gunpoint—"

He winced.

"Oh yeah, I'm not letting that go anytime soon. Maybe ever." That infectious grin was back, her full lips in a wide smile. "And now you're peppering me with a lot of super personal questions so you get to tell me everything about Ellis Bishop that I ask."

He couldn't help but smile. God, he hadn't smiled in months. Everything had been about surviving and getting to the truth—still was. But Arianna, the real her, was a breath of fresh air. She was all energy and sunshine and it was messing with his head. "That's more than fair. What do you want to know?"

She tapped her lips once and he forced his gaze not to stray to them. "Let's see. Okay, so your family is pretty wealthy. Which I would never normally say to someone, but again, kidnapper, so...how did you end up working for the DEA? I imagine you could have gone to work for your family's company and had a nice, cushy desk job."

"Man, you just get right to it," he murmured, though he was glad she wasn't holding back. He really, really loved this side of her. And hated himself more than a little bit right then, for ever thinking badly of her. "I was in the Marines years ago." More years than he wanted to think about, especially since he was thirty-seven, more than a decade older than her. "When I got out, a couple buddies didn't make the transition to civilian life well and got caught up in drugs. It happened so fast too. Drugs, heroin mainly, ruined their lives... And not just theirs, but it screwed up their families too."

She simply nodded, truly listening.

"One thing led to another, and when I was graduating college I put in an application with the DEA. Honestly I was surprised to get hired without any law enforcement experience. But with my background in the Marines and my criminal justice degree, they scooped me up. Good timing more than anything."

"Undercover work, right?"

"Not at first, no. I did a lot of grunt work in the beginning. But yeah, it evolved into that eventually."

"I'm kinda surprised you're working so close to where your family lives."

He smiled faintly at her insight. "I normally work on the West Coast and...other places. I was working in Orlando for my last job because I was on the periphery of the actual job and there wasn't much of a risk of someone recognizing me. And Carter and I had worked so often together before that it made sense for us to team up. It was supposed to be a small part of a much bigger operation. Then when Carter got killed..." Lifting a shoulder, he looked away.

"I'm sorry about your friend. Truly."

"Thanks." He cleared his throat. "Now how about something lighter for conversation?"

"All right, then. Any girlfriends or a wife you left behind when you went on the run? I didn't actually pay much attention to the news and I haven't had a chance to stalk you online yet."

He snickered. "No, no one. Doing undercover work doesn't leave a lot of room for relationships. Not healthy ones, anyway."

"Oh, I bet."

"I don't plan on doing this long term though. You know, if I manage to clear my name," he said dryly.

Which made her laugh lightly, as he'd intended. "Really?"

"Yeah. Before everything blew up in my face, I'd been thinking seriously about getting out. I'd even put out a few feelers before...just before." God, he hated thinking about Carter being gone. It cut too deep.

"Well, when you clear your name people are going to be desperate to hire you, because you know this is going to make the news. You'll be famous for fifteen minutes and get name recognition for good things."

"You've got a lot of faith in that outcome."

She ran her hand through her dark hair and shrugged. "I'm just trying to stay positive. I've found that it makes

96 | KATIE REUS

things easier in general. I'm trying not to let my mind wander and get sucked into...well, into what's going to happen if everything goes sideways. There are so many things that could just pull me under right now, so I tend to make jokes to make things easier on myself. It's either that or get pulled into a black hole of doom and gloom. You know?"

No, he didn't because he'd been living day to day the last few months and focusing on the negative, but he nodded because he wanted to please her.

And that was a strange revelation. One he wasn't sure what to do with.

CHAPTER EIGHT

Arianna jumped to her feet when there was a sharp rap on the stateroom door. They'd stopped not too long ago and had been waiting for the go-ahead that they could disembark.

Ellis stood as well, his movements liquid grace. "We've got a few minutes."

He'd warned her that when they docked, their boat might be checked, so the two of them were going to hide in a secret cubby in the closet. She was curious why it even existed, though could more or less gauge the reason. *To hide stuff.*

She wasn't sure who was helping them, just that one of his friends was apparently super rich. Yeah she knew his family was wealthy, but owning a yacht was a totally different kind of wealth.

Like one-percent crazy money.

Ellis opened the closet door, his broad shoulders filling up the sleek, teakwood frame. When he stepped farther inside, she followed after him. It was already cramped but then he pressed something on the wall—a button of some kind she couldn't see—and the panel slid back to reveal a small, carpeted space that would fit two standing people. Barely.

He stepped in first and pressed back against the wall.

She moved in after him, plastering her body to his because there was no other choice. He was rock-hard against her, all lean muscles and raw strength. And good God, the man was tall and built. She'd known it, but being in the enclosed space really drove home that point.

"It's going to get dark in here, but it won't be for long." His deep voice was all soothing and gentle. Very different from when he'd first kidnapped her. Just the sound of his voice did strange things to her insides—things she was going to ignore. "And if things go sideways, just act like you're here against your will."

"Okay," she said quietly, trying to ignore how good he smelled. It was hard when her face was right up against his chest. That masculine, dark scent she was coming to associate with him wrapped around her, making her light-headed, and she leaned even closer against him.

He pressed a section of a small double hook that looked as if it could be used for hanging hats or robes. As soon as he did, the wall slid back into place with a faint swishing sound.

The architecture of this was incredible, and if he hadn't told her about the buttons earlier, she never would have seen either one. She wondered if this storage area was for smuggling cigars or something.

As she shifted against him, she tried really hard not to be aware of all of his sleek muscles and rock-hard body against her. She thought the sexual part of her had not only died, but withered away years ago. Around Ellis it was coming to life with a vengeance. Which was so inappropriate, and really, the worst timing ever.

She hadn't been with anybody since she'd gotten completely sober, had turned down so many dates she couldn't count. It was as if men knew she wasn't interested so they came out in droves or something.

She simply didn't want to get to know anybody because eventually it would lead to getting naked. And she was terrified of what that entailed.

She wasn't sure she could have sex sober. Or good sex. *Ugh.*

Closing her eyes even though it was dark, she laid her cheek against his chest and took a steadying breath. He smelled spicy, something masculine that she was still trying to pin down. Whatever it was, she liked it as much as she liked the feel of his hard chest against her. The man might have kidnapped her originally, but right now she felt strangely safe with him. Bonded, almost. And when he'd kidnapped her, he'd gone out of his way to be gentle with her, even when he'd thought she was a monster. He could have done anything he wanted, but when she'd brought up rape, he'd been so disgusted and horrified.

He shifted slightly, moving a fraction as he settled his big hands on her hips. And oh, wow, she liked the feel of his hands on her—way too much.

Something she would not have thought twenty-four hours ago. She'd been surprised how easygoing and apologetic Ellis had been. Well, not the apologetic part—she'd expected that after what he'd done—but he'd been so sincere, so horrified at himself, that she'd made the decision to simply forgive him. Even after his original apology, he'd kept saying he was sorry.

More often than not she found herself letting little things go with people because it was easier to live her life that way. But what he'd done was horrible and huge. Still, she knew he'd done it for what he thought were the right reasons and he hadn't hurt her or taken advantage. Hadn't even wanted her to come down here once he realized she was innocent. He seemed so averse to the idea, and damn, that heartfelt apology he'd given had melted her a little. Which was ridiculous.

She was being ridiculous. *Gah!* She needed to stop thinking about him. She shoved all her thoughts back down, willing herself not to think of Ellis Bishop in any sort of sexual way. They were simply working together for a common goal. And even though she knew she shouldn't invest emotional energy in the outcome of his current situation, she found she cared very much that he was on the run after being falsely accused of killing someone. His best friend.

It was clear he was hurting every time he talked and looked at her. And yeah, she cared because she wasn't a robot. She wanted this man to get his life back.

"Sorry," he murmured, so softly she barely heard him.

She started to ask him what he was sorry for, then she shifted slightly against him and realized he had an erection.

Arianna froze in shock, not that she could do much otherwise. She'd read that under intense situations people's bodies reacted differently, so he must be really stressed right now. She'd been so caught up in her head that she hadn't even noticed, but now it was all she could focus on. That thick length between them.

And, wow. She couldn't respond at this point so she remained still and tried to focus on anything but that. But it was impossible.

He wasn't attracted to her, he couldn't be—or she didn't think so. He hadn't given any outward signs of that. But of course he wouldn't, because he'd literally kidnapped her and then what was he going to do, hit on her?

Stop thinking about this, she ordered herself. She had way more important things to focus on. Like the next step after they went to that bank and she found out whether or not those accounts were real or not.

She really didn't want them to be real, wanted all of this to be a giant mistake. But deep down she didn't think it was. She'd read those emails from whoever had sent him more files and it was looking more and more like someone—very likely her stepfather—had done this to her.

She'd worry about what to do after they got to the bank. One step, one day at a time. She lived that mantra.

She shifted her feet slightly when she heard low murmured voices nearby. Then she froze, digging her fingers into his shoulders as they stood there. If possible, she would step back and give him space but there simply wasn't anywhere to go. They were squished in here.

What would happen if someone discovered them? Oh God, she hadn't even thought that far ahead. She'd just been so focused on hiding here and then Ellis's very clear erection that she hadn't even thought what would happen if they were caught.

He'd told her he'd admit to kidnapping her, but if he went to jail, he was certain he'd be killed before a trial. He said that was why he'd been on the run and trying to clear his name.

Stop stressing out, she ordered herself. She always did this, and she was really glad he couldn't read her mind because she was a hot mess up in there.

At the sound of a very specific rap on the door, Ellis waited a minute and then pressed the button, opening the door.

Sucking in a big breath, she stepped out, turning away from him and hurrying out of the small closet. It was like sensory overload as she got out of that small, dark space and into the bright, plush room. The bedcovers were slightly rumpled and the food mostly eaten. Anyone looking at the room would assume the owner had been using this space, so nothing was out of the ordinary. Her heart was still an erratic drumbeat in her chest, but she could breathe easier at least now that they were no longer plastered against each other.

"We'll wait until we get another knock on the door," he said quietly, avoiding her gaze.

"Sounds good."

From here they would be going to a private airstrip and taking a flight to Grand Cayman Island. From there... She had to face reality. She would have to go to the bank. Something she wasn't looking forward to.

"I'm sorry about in there," he muttered, still refusing to look at her. "Stress reaction."

"Yeah, I figured that's what it was." Her voice was a little too high-pitched. She inwardly winced but didn't look at him. She didn't want to make him feel bad about it. They needed to simply move past it and pretend it hadn't happened.

Still, she had to force herself not to think about how impressive his thick length had felt against her lower abdomen, about how curious she was to see more of him. *Oh, no. Noooo.* This was not good. She hadn't felt any sort of sexual curiosity or been aroused in so long that the sensation was foreign.

She didn't know what to do with these alarming feelings.

CHAPTER NINE

An hour later Arianna sat on a white leather couch in a nondescript condo with beige tile, beige walls and cheap-looking tropical-themed art. Though the word "art" was definitely a stretch. She was glad to finally be stopped somewhere after riding on a yacht, then a small boat to another marina, then a short car ride to a private airstrip. And then finally they'd flown in a very plush private plane to Grand Cayman.

Her skin was cold even though sweat beaded across her forehead. She felt clammy and knew she must look pale given Ellis's concerned expression. They'd just arrived at this place so they could prep before heading to the bank.

The reality of everything was crashing in on her in a sweeping wave. She looked away from him as she dragged in a deep breath.

Before she could take another one, he'd crouched down in front of her, taking her hands in his. "We can turn around and leave."

She squeezed his hands, feeling the little calluses and taking the comfort he was offering because she desperately needed it. "You've got to stop doing that."

He frowned, that little dent between his brows growing deeper. "Doing what?"

"Offering to leave every time I stress out."

He held her hands gently. "I just want to remind you that the option is still there. I want to clear my name, but not at the cost of hurting you."

Good God, how did he know that was the perfect thing to say? Her gaze trailed down to his lips and she swallowed hard. She'd never been into guys with beards before, but it looked far too sexy on him.

She closed her eyes and took a deep breath. "We are definitely doing this. I'm just not used to feeling so out of control. I work with third graders every day." She let out a nervous laugh as she met his gaze again.

He still hadn't backed away and continued to hold her hands so very gently in his much bigger ones. And damn, did she like it. He was such a soothing, steady presence.

"Well I think you're pretty incredible," he said quietly. And when his gaze landed on her mouth, that was definitely raw heat that flashed in his eyes.

Oh, she liked that. Without thinking, she licked her suddenly dry lips.

Abruptly he dropped her hands as if she'd burned him and stood, nearly bumping into the bamboo coffee table behind him. Clearing his throat, he'd put a few feet of distance between them before she could blink.

Okay, then. At least one of them was thinking clearly.

"The good thing is," he said as he shifted one of the long, vertical blinds over the sliding glass door to the side. "We can still make the scene at your house work for us if you change your mind about going to the bank. I can just give Vitaly a ransom note and we can go from there. You don't have to get any further involved in this."

"No. I need to see for myself if those accounts are in my name. I have to know." Finding her center—and really wishing she could call her sponsor—she stood on steady feet. "And we need to get there before the bank closes. I don't want to be here another day."

Though his expression was pinched, he nodded. "Let's do this, then. The clothes are in the bedroom."

She wasn't sure where he'd gotten clothes from but he'd apparently thought of everything, and when they'd arrived at this nondescript condo in a slightly run-down complex, everything had been waiting for them. Whoever was helping Ellis—and she definitely had some guesses on who—was loaded. Which told her that with all these resources, Ellis Bishop could have left the country and started over somewhere new with ease. He would have been able to blend in and flourish. Sure, he'd have needed to leave his family. But he'd be alive and could start over.

A guilty man didn't go back to the scene of the crime and hang out for months while trying to solve it. No, he hadn't killed his partner, and something very wrong was going on with her stepfather. Something that apparently involved her. She was doing this today.

She was going to help Ellis clear his name even if that meant Vitaly went to prison.

Inside the bedroom, she stared at the clothing that had been laid out for her, a forest green dress of fine material that would make her eyes pop. As she held it up, she saw the brand and her eyes widened.

To complete the look were jaguar-printed suede Louboutin spiked heels that had a teeny tiny ankle strap and a bigger one that went right over the top of her foot. The little gold spikes on the strap added sparkle to it and she decided right then that if she survived this, she was keeping these damn shoes.

After applying a few coats of mascara and lip gloss, she stood in her new ensemble in front of a mirror and understood why Ellis had wanted her to change. She needed to look like a million freaking dollars when going in to close a million-dollar-plus account at the bank. And right now, in the formfitting, expensive dress and shoes, she looked like the kind of woman who didn't take shit from anyone.

So even if she was a quaking mess on the inside, she was going to do this.

She was going to close out a bank account worth millions of dollars and start getting some damn answers.

CHAPTER TEN

Ellis turned at the sound of the car's passenger door opening, nearly going for his weapon until Evie said, "It's just me."

In disguise as a middle-aged man with a slight paunch wearing khaki pants, Birkenstocks and a loose button-down shirt with wild Hawaiian flowers, she looked nothing like his sister—or a woman. Her experience in spycraft was definitely useful today.

"Holy shit," he murmured before turning back to the entrance of the bank. She'd told him she'd be coming to him in disguise but he hadn't expected anything like this. "Where's Dylan?"

"Around," she said vaguely. Dylan and Evie had flown here on another private plane owned by one of Dylan's friends.

Parked across the street in a pay-by-the-hour parking lot strategically out of the way of most cameras, he was keeping an eye on the front of the bank for Arianna. He'd contemplated going inside the bank with her but she had a burner phone on her and had called his phone, so he was currently listening to everything through his Bluetooth. Everything sounded normal so far and he didn't have reason to believe anything would go wrong. But he was ready to run with her if it did.

"How's she doing?" Evie asked quietly.

"Good. She can't hear me, but I can hear her. She left her phone in her purse but she's not wearing an earpiece." He'd thought it might look too suspicious.

His sister nodded. "I'm impressed that she's doing this."

"Me too."

"You think she's going to betray you?"

He'd asked himself that question a hundred times. "No. I don't. At this point nothing would surprise me, but my instinct is telling me I can trust her."

"Well her online life and all her movements in life say the same. She's nothing like her father." Lizzy had sent Ellis more information and he'd shared it with his sister—who'd then done some research of her own.

"Stepfather," he muttered.

"How's she holding up? With you, I mean. Like on the boat ride over here?" Evie asked.

He wished Evie could have met Arianna but he still wanted his sister and Dylan separated from her. He might trust Arianna, but his sister's safety was paramount. After everything his family had been through recently, he wasn't making any of them targets again.

"She's tough. Tougher than I expected." He had a feeling that her being a recovering alcoholic had a whole lot to do with it. "She's holding up better than some of the newbies at work." And he couldn't help but be impressed by that.

"You like her," his sister blurted. When he raised his eyebrows, she gave him a pointed look, her eyes narrowed slightly under the ball cap, makeup and short wig.

He shrugged. "Doesn't matter if I do."

"Are you kidding me? You cannot get involved with her right now."

He turned away from her, watching the bank again. "You think I don't know that?" Ellis wasn't going to make a move on her or do anything stupid. Back in the secret hideaway on the yacht, he'd been so tempted to kiss her but it would've been a mistake of epic proportion. Getting romantically involved with a woman he was depending on to help clear his name? *No.*

"Just make sure you remember what's at stake right now."

He didn't bother looking at her, focused on keeping an eye out for Arianna. And if he was being honest, some deep part of him was craving seeing her again. "You think I can forget? I've been living in hiding for months."

"Yeah I know. I'm sorry."

Ellis had missed her wedding and he hated that. Evie was his little sister—he should have been there. And he hadn't been there for his brother Evan after he'd been nearly killed in a bombing that had scarred him and put him in a coma. It was a miracle Evan was alive. So yeah, he knew what was at stake. His whole life.

"Look, I'll make sure that none of this falls back on Arianna," Evie said. "No matter what happens, she's not going to get dragged down by her stepfather."

"Thank you." Ellis couldn't control what happened to him, and if he got killed, he wanted to know that someone was looking out for Arianna. It wasn't just about him anymore. She was in this now too, and he'd realized that he couldn't keep working alone anymore. He needed help if he was going to bring down Vitaly and his former boss—and anyone else involved in this mess.

"Showtime." Ellis started the car as Arianna stepped out of the bank into the waning sunlight.

Though he was across the street, he nearly sucked in a breath at the sight of her. Wearing a knee-length, formfitting green dress that looked tailor-made for her sweet curves, and the spiked heels his sister had somehow procured, she looked like a million bucks. Her long, dark hair was down around her shoulders in soft waves, the breeze blowing it away from her face as she moved in smooth, sinuous strides. Damn, it was hard to breathe right now.

"I'll see you later." Evie ducked out of the car, making a hasty exit across the parking lot before Arianna reached them.

There was no way Arianna would be able to put Evie together with that middle-aged man, but he understood Evie's need to work in the shadows regardless.

"Any problems?" he asked as Arianna slid into the passenger seat, even though he'd been listening through his earpiece. It had been all mundane paperwork.

"No problems. They were surprised I was closing the account but they couldn't do anything about it when I had my ID." She let out a shaky breath and leaned back in the seat. The windows were darkly tinted, obscuring anyone's attempt to look inside. Not that anyone was paying attention to them.

A few tourists strolled along the street in front of them as he pulled out of the parking lot. There was little traffic this time of day, the red, Mediterranean-style roofs of the nearby shops casting shadows under the setting sun.

"It's possible that someone at the bank will be contacting your stepfather if he was directly involved with opening the account." They'd already been over this, but he liked to think out loud. Her stepfather either had someone on his payroll at the bank, who'd opened the account in her name, or more likely he'd used someone who looked very similar to her to open it. Ellis was betting on the latter given the travel records in Arianna's name that he'd discovered.

"I know." She sighed and looked out the window at a two-story restaurant with purple, peach and green-painted walls with a huge neon sign that proclaimed *Cheap Margaritas*.

Next door was a building with bright blue walls and a neon sign advertising *Shirts and Souvenirs*. God, this place was such a tourist trap.

"Who was that who left the vehicle before I got in?" she asked quietly.

"Someone helping us."

"You won't tell me who?"

He slid his sunglasses on as he turned directly into the setting sun. "I don't want to lie to you."

"Fair enough. I'm keeping these shoes, by the way."

He let out a snort, surprised by her words. Though maybe he shouldn't be after getting to know her a bit. At the next light he took a left turn and passed a set of orange buildings with various international flags and plants hanging off the second-story balconies.

"So what happens now with the check?" She was starting to fidget again.

"We're going to hold on to it." They weren't doing anything with those funds other than keeping them secure until he could get to Vitaly.

"At your safe house?" she asked, watching him carefully.

He could hear the note of worry in her voice. "I think we should put it somewhere. Not at your house, but I'll do what you want. You have a stake in all this too."

At his answer, she shoved out a breath. "I don't want it. And I definitely don't want it at my house." She shuddered and wrapped her arms around herself.

He took another turn onto a two-lane highway lined with palm trees and blue-green water stretching out for miles on the right side of them. "When we get to the airfield, I'm going to have to put a pistol on you. It's not loaded. But—"

"Ellis, I know all this. We've gone over this part already."

He liked the exasperated way she said his name. His real name, not asshole or Mr. Kidnapper. "I know. I just...don't like the idea of putting a weapon on you."

"Believe me, I'm glad you don't like the thought of hurting me or even the appearance of hurting me. Are you going to wear a mask?" She half turned, looking at the clothing he'd tossed into the back of the car.

"I don't want him to know it's me just yet. And he'll be able to pull feeds from this airport." Which was why they were leaving from it. He wanted Vitaly to see the recordings, wanted to see him forcing Arianna onto the plane against her will. He didn't want there to be any hint that she had done any of this willingly. She needed to be a victim if she was going to avoid her stepfather's wrath. "I need to figure out who else might be working with him other than my former boss. But we'll find out in the next twenty-four hours, I'm sure."

She simply nodded because they'd gone over those details too. Though he hadn't told her exactly how he was going to find out. Because once she got to that part of the operation, he knew she was going to be annoyed with him. And he'd decided to hold off as long as possible because of that. She didn't hate him anymore and he found that mattered to him far too much.

"Is anyone else flying back with us?"

"Other than the pilot, no. And he's been paid very handsomely to do this."

She nodded. "What if my stepfather figures out who the pilot is though? He'll know this guy flew us and saw you holding a gun on me."

"We've already thought of that. As soon as he lands in Miami, he's going to be taking a vacation until all this is settled."

She let out a breath and leaned back against her seat. "Good. I don't want anyone's blood on my hands."

He liked that she was worried about other people, a man she didn't even know. Which lined up with what he'd learned about the real Arianna. "So teacher of the year, huh?" he asked, wanting to talk about anything other than what they were currently doing.

"What?" She shifted against the seat and crossed her legs toward him.

He forced himself not to look at her sleek, bronze-toned calves—tried not to imagine what it would feel like to have them thrown over his shoulders or wrapped around his hips. "When I was researching you, I found out that you were teacher of the year last year. That's pretty impressive."

She lifted a shoulder, clearly uncomfortable with the praise. "Just at my school. It's not like it was a national award or anything."

"Still impressive," he murmured. Everything about her was.

CHAPTER ELEVEN

"You look creepy," Arianna said as they walked across the tarmac. She knew that somehow Ellis had cleared out this area of the private airport. Or whoever he was working with had taken care of it.

Which just drove home the point that if he wanted, he really could disappear forever. He had wealthy friends, clearly, and his family was loaded too. But he wanted Vitaly to pay for murdering his friend and that said a lot about who Ellis was as a man.

"I know," he muttered. He had on one of those creepy white Halloween masks and was wearing a mechanic-type jumpsuit that covered everything except his gloved hands.

She was still in her dress and wearing the uncomfortable but gorgeous heels, which were probably slowing them down.

"We're coming up on the camera. Keep looking down," he said. "Look afraid."

She kept her gaze on the asphalt as they strode forward. Gripping her upper arm, he dragged her forward and moved the unloaded gun away from her back, likely so that wherever the camera was got a good glimpse of it.

She stumbled a few times, which probably looked great for the security feeds. Once they were inside the plane, Ellis stripped off his mask and she stepped out of her shoes, stretching her toes. Anxiety still settled in her gut, but being in the private plane alone with Ellis eased some of it. They'd gotten one huge step out of the way and she was trying really hard not to think about what would happen once they got back to Miami.

One step at a time.

Ellis started stripping out of the jumpsuit as the pilot joined them in the cabin. As the two men spoke in low tones, Arianna grabbed a plush robe from the bathroom and put it on over her dress before moving to the mini-bar and pouring herself a glass of sparkling water. The dress was super tight, and while it was gorgeous, she felt weird wearing something so revealing and uncomfortable. Something about the robe made her feel like she had "armor" against the rest of the world. Also, it was comfortable and felt like she had a big blanket wrapped around her. It gave her a strange sort of comfort.

"We're about to head out," Ellis said as he sat across from her. "Nice robe."

She half-smiled, even as nerves still danced in her belly. And not the good kind. "Is everything good with the pilot?"

"Yeah. There's going to be a vehicle waiting for us when we land and we'll be disembarking inside a warehouse with no cameras. And he's going to be leaving directly from there, heading to I don't want to know where."

"Good."

"Why don't you try to get some sleep? You've had a stressful, long day."

Yeah, she had. Being in the bank, dealing with all of that by herself had been…weird. She'd kept expecting them to call her out on being a liar and get security. And she knew that her troubles were just beginning because very soon her stepfather would know his money was gone. Or she assumed he would. "I don't think I can sleep. I'm too wired."

"I get it. You mind if I make some calls?" He was watching her carefully and being oh so polite. Probably because he felt guilty about holding a gun on her and dragging her along the tarmac.

"Do whatever you need to do." She knew things weren't over now that she'd closed the account.

No, they were just beginning.

Even though she said she couldn't sleep, she closed her eyes as the engine rumbled and the pilot started announcing that they needed to strap in, blah, blah, blah. "I'm keeping this robe too," she murmured. It would be a souvenir of the weirdest day she'd ever had. And also a reminder of Ellis, the sexiest man she'd ever known.

Ellis just chuckled. "That's fine."

As they took off, she leaned her seat back and closed her eyes. With Ellis next to her, talking in low tones, she let sleep pull her under.

* * *

"I know we've been over this, but I just want to re-mind you that it won't be real." Ellis's deep voice cut through Arianna's thoughts and the interior of the non-descript truck. She had no idea who the vehicle belonged to, but just as he'd said, it had been waiting for them at the airport. It had darkly tinted windows and was maybe a decade old, but the paint job was nice. It smelled like the April spring air freshener hanging on the rearview mirror, and it had clearly been taken care of.

She still couldn't believe she'd fallen asleep for most of the plane ride to Miami. Although maybe she shouldn't be surprised, because when she was asleep she didn't have to think about the ramifications of what she'd done—what she was taking part in. Or the fact that she now had a check in her purse for a few million dollars. She wondered if her stepfather or whoever had set up the account knew it had been closed. The bank employee who'd helped her close the account had *not* been happy with her, but he hadn't been able to argue with her since her name and signature were on file and no one else's.

Now she and Ellis were driving toward an unknown destination, though she knew what was going to happen when they got there. She just hoped that pilot really did skip town for a while.

"I know," she said. "We've been over it." It wasn't like she was looking forward to him taking a picture that made it look like she was being held hostage, but it was the only way her stepfather wouldn't think she was will-ingly involved. And hopefully it would bring Ellis that much closer to his goal of getting his life back.

Internally Arianna was still battling the knowledge that her stepfather had almost a hundred percent been behind opening this and other accounts in her name. He had all her personal information and her signature on file from various paperwork she'd signed after her mother's death. It was definitely in the realm of possibility. And Ellis swore that Vitaly had killed his partner—and she believed him. Which was a very weird knowledge to have.

"I can send a message to him without a picture of you." Ellis put the truck into park as he stopped outside a big warehouse with bright orange and green graffiti on the outside.

"No. This will work better with the picture and you know it." Instead of looking at him, she scanned their surroundings. The parking lot stretched out in both directions and the warehouse itself looked quiet, almost abandoned. She supposed there could be people inside, but there was a thick padlock on the only door she could see from the vehicle.

Without waiting for him to respond, she opened the door and slid out. The air smelled of salt, thicker than normal, so she knew they must be close to the water.

She didn't like being restrained again, as she knew she'd have to be for the picture, but it was only going to be for a few minutes. Ellis was going to send Vitaly a nasty message along with a picture of her gagged and tied up to drive home the point that he wasn't fucking around.

"You just better make sure the gag isn't dirty," she muttered, finally looking at Ellis as they met in front of the truck.

Holding on to a small duffel bag, he let out a startled laugh and she found that she liked his laughter way too much. He'd only laughed a couple times since their very unusual "meeting" and she felt all warm inside when he did. She shouldn't have any feelings whatsoever for this man, but apparently her head and heart were dumbasses.

"Should we tear my dress a little bit? Maybe mess up my hair?" That way it would make it look good. "Just don't ruin my shoes. Like I said, I'm keeping them."

He stared at her in surprise and maybe a little horror as he unlocked the padlock.

"What? You want to sell this, don't you?"

"I do. I just...I don't like any of this." He pushed the door open, his frown deepening.

"Ellis, this was your idea. You're the one taking the pictures!"

"I know. I still don't have to like it," he growled.

Actually growled. And for some reason it sounded sexy. *Uh oh. No, no, no.* Not sexy. She followed him inside, fighting a shiver as he shut the door behind them.

For a brief moment blackness reigned until he flipped on a light to reveal... Nothing. A faint whining sound of the fluorescent lights filled the air as they flipped on, one by one, illuminating the empty warehouse. It was a fairly small one but there weren't any boxes or anything anyone could hide behind. "What is this place?"

"I honestly don't know. Someone is letting me use it."
Ellis looked around too, inspecting what little there was
to see.

"Your mysterious yacht owner?" she asked, beyond
curious who owned that boat. And the private plane, for
that matter.

"No. Someone else."

"You really could just disappear and start over in another country, couldn't you?" She phrased it as a question
even though she knew the answer.

"Yeah, but I'm not going to. I'm going to clear my
name." His words were a vow.

"What happens if you can't?" She was a realist and
knew that things didn't always end up the way they
should. The good guys didn't always win, unfortunately.
All you had to do was turn on the news to know that.
She thought of all the corrupt politicians who got away
with so much all the time. Lies stacked upon lies. It was
like an avalanche of crap coming at you every day.

"I'll cross that bridge if I get to it." He tightened his
jaw and looked down at her. "Ripping your dress was a
good idea. So maybe you want to..." He trailed off and
looked away again.

She looked down at the pretty dress and tried to figure out where exactly to rip it. Finally she just grabbed
onto the scoop neck and tugged... And all she managed
was stretching it out awkwardly. "Pretty sure you're going to have to do this for me. And for the record, I'm sad
about this dress. Really, really sad, because it's gorgeous."

He frowned down at her, his pale eyes darkening.

"I'm sorry I have spaghetti noodle arms and no muscles," she said, rolling her eyes. "You're gonna have to do it."

His mouth quirked up. "You don't have spaghetti noodle arms." His eyes flared with the barest hint of heat before he cleared his throat. "Fine," he muttered before he carefully reached for the front of her dress. In one quick action, he tore the front, pulling it apart as if it was made of paper. It exposed her bra all the way down to her belly button.

Which just made her feel that much weaker. Also, his display of strength? Totally not sexy. Nope. Not at all. "Wow, I really do need to start going back to the gym." Her instinct was to cover herself, but that wouldn't work for the picture so she just pretended that her bra wasn't showing. The thing covered more than most bikinis so it really wasn't that big of a deal—at least that was what she tried to tell herself.

He simply shook his head, very studiously avoiding looking at her exposed bra. "If you want to do something to your hair, go for it. I'm going to set things up."

She nodded and flipped her head over and started finger combing her hair and teasing it, making it as wild as possible. She needed to look like a mistreated captive, one who'd been forced to close a bank account, then do God only knew what else at gunpoint.

When she flipped her head back up, she saw that he was setting up a chair and a black tarp behind it. Whoever owned this warehouse must have left it for him. The tarp made sense—there would be nothing in the background of the picture. Just her. And he'd told her that he planned to strip all the metadata from the image so Vitaly wouldn't be able to figure out where it had been taken. Though she guessed it really wouldn't matter at this point because they weren't staying here afterward.

"I'm ready when you are." Ellis's voice echoed in the vast emptiness of the warehouse.

She was still wearing the gorgeous heels, and her shoes clicked across the concrete as she made her way toward him. Then she sat in the chair and waited as he tied down her wrists. For a brief moment she tensed at the sensation of being tied up, but this was Ellis. She trusted him. He took one of her shoes when he was done.

"Hey!"

"It's just temporary. It'll look better if you only have one shoe." His lips curved up in a sort of smile as he looked up at her from his crouched position.

And seriously the man was so damn sexy right now. Which made her feel all kinds of screwed up in the head for noticing.

But spending time with him, being around the completely driven man, had somehow opened up something sensual and hungry inside her she thought was long dead. It was...disturbing.

His blue eyes dilated slightly as he looked at her, and when his gaze fell to her mouth, her belly tightened. She was pretty sure he liked what he saw when he looked at her.

She wondered what it would feel like to have his full mouth on hers. Would he be gentle or would he just take what he wanted, stealing her breath? She didn't know which one she would like better. Both.

Ellis looked away before she could contemplate more, snagging his camera. "Look angry. Look like you did when I..." He trailed off but she knew what he'd been about to say.

"When you kidnapped me and I was fantasizing about stabbing you in the head?"

His lips twitched. "Yes, exactly."

"Wait, what about the gag?"

"I think it works better without it."

Okay, then. It felt weird but she did what he said, glaring at the camera in pure defiance as he snapped a few pictures.

It was done so quickly. A few snaps, then he released her restraints. Though she'd known it was temporary, a weird frisson of relief slid through her to be free. She didn't like feeling vulnerable, unable to defend herself from anything.

To her surprise, Ellis gently took her calf as he slid her shoe back onto her foot. She sucked in a very slight breath at the feel of his big, callused hand on her bare skin. It was hard not to wonder what it would feel like to have that big hand sliding over other places...cupping her, teasing her, stroking her.

She nearly jolted back at the erotic thought. She really had thought that part of her was dead. But now her former kidnapper was turning her on. Something must be wrong with her. *Maybe Stockholm syndrome*, she thought, but she wasn't a prisoner anymore, so she didn't even have that as an excuse.

She just really, really liked him.

"Once I press send, there's no turning back." Ellis held the burner phone in his hand as they stood outside the warehouse.

She took the phone from his hands and looked at the pictures he'd attached to the draft text message. She looked truly pissed off, her dark hair wild and tangled, and with her dress ripped and missing a shoe—he'd definitely been right about the shoe—this looked real. She pressed send.

"Well then, I guess there's no turning back."

She simply handed him the phone and he typed in a message.

"'I've got your daughter and your money,'" Ellis said. "That should about cover it."

Yep, that did. Stomach tight with anxiety, she pulled open the passenger side of the truck as he smashed the phone underneath his boot.

"Now we head back to a safe house," he said.

.

CHAPTER TWELVE

Nearly twenty minutes later they were back at the safe house he'd originally taken her to, and this time Arianna had been allowed to see where they were going—though she'd stayed in the back seat in case her stepfather was running any sort of facial recognition software programs. Ellis said that since he had a beard and was wearing a ball cap that covered his ears, nothing should pick him up. He was more worried about the FBI finding him than Vitaly anyway.

"You need to get better food here," she said as they settled into the makeshift office he'd set up. He'd given her a shirt to put on over her ripped dress and she liked that it smelled like Ellis. "Hey," she said before he could respond, staring at the camera feed that very clearly showed four different angles of the exterior of her home. "Is that my house?"

Ellis cut her a sideways glance, looking almost sheepish. "Yeah, I didn't want to tell you about this."

"How do you have cameras outside my house? And... Oh, this is from when you were stalking me!" Sighing, she sat back in the chair next to him.

He slightly shifted the laptop so she could get a better view. "Yeah, guilty as charged."

"I can't believe I didn't see the cameras."

"They're microcameras and impossible to see even for someone who knows they're there. You would have had to stumble on them accidentally."

"Is this why you didn't tell me what we were going to be doing tonight?"

He lifted a shoulder. "Figured you already hated me for so much, so I wasn't going to pile on even more reasons."

"I don't hate you. I think what you did was really messed up, but I don't hate you. And you're the one running for your life. I can only imagine what I would do in that situation." She had a feeling she'd cross a whole lot of lines to get her life back if it had been taken from her.

"I'm so sorry for what I did," he said quietly, looking away from her, his jaw tight. "And I will take responsibility for it."

The man was so heartbreakingly sexy she found it hard not to watch him instead of the laptop. "You can stop apologizing. So, what are we looking for?" She reached for a bag of chips he'd set on the table. Freaking Fritos. Who the heck ate Fritos without dip or chili? But she was hungry, so apparently she did.

"Vitaly is going to want to confirm that you've been taken. I mean yeah, he's got the proof, but he's going to start checking all the bank accounts and send someone to your house to confirm."

"Okay, so then what?"

"First I want to see who comes by your house. I want to see if it's just men who work for him, or someone else."

"You mean like...your former boss or something?"

He nodded. "Yeah. And I'm recording your house for the future."

"That's good at least."

He nodded, his gaze straying back to the laptop.

She snuck a peek at him out of the corner of her eye, then inwardly cursed herself. She found herself looking at him more and more. Those pale blue eyes were etched into her mind. Especially the way he occasionally watched her with a barely concealed longing.

He was wrong about her hating him—she definitely didn't hate him. In fact, she was far too attracted to him for her own comfort. This entire situation was insane, and sex or anything in that realm should not be on her mind. But...she couldn't seem to get it out of her mind. It wouldn't be a relationship or anything like that. No, it would be temporary and maybe that was a good thing. With Ellis she was herself because there was no pretending around this man. And she trusted him. Which, again, was so strange. So she was attracted to him and trusted him. Maybe, just maybe, a one- or two-night fling would be kind of amazing. Or crazy. She couldn't decide.

"So what's up with the Fritos?" She kept her gaze on the camera feed, watching absolutely nothing but her front porch. Her little snowman on the top step was still in place and the all-season planter swayed slightly in the breeze.

"What about them?"

"Do you actually eat them without dip?"

"They're good." His tone was slightly defensive.

She snorted. "I'm feeling edgy so I'm eating, but eating lone Fritos is kinda weird."

"You sound like my sister," he muttered. "You would definitely like her."

Arianna wondered if she'd ever get to meet his family but shoved that thought away. Right now she was forcing herself to take things one step at a time.

"I've got more snacks downstairs," he continued before she could respond. Then he straightened as two figures moved onto the screen. "Damn, that didn't take long," he murmured as he leaned forward slightly.

Tossing the Fritos onto the desk, she watched alongside him, not recognizing the two men who strode up to her front door and knocked.

Ellis typed in a few commands on-screen, changing the angle, and she got a clear view of both their faces. She nearly jerked back in surprise at what a close-up shot it was. The camera had to be somewhere on her door frame.

He let out a low, savage curse.

"What?" she asked.

"I recognize both these guys. One works for your stepfather and the other is a DEA agent. I haven't worked with him in years, but I know him. So that's at least two agents on Vitaly's payroll," he muttered and she got the feeling the last part was more to himself than her.

Reaching out, she gently squeezed his knee. "I'm sorry." It had to be hard on him to know that people he should be able to trust had turned out to be traitors. She herself didn't have much faith in law enforcement but it was clear that he did and this had to be even harder for him. He was on the run and in hiding because of corrupt assholes. She wanted to help him more than ever.

He placed his hand over hers, wrapped his callused fingers around hers and squeezed.

And God help her, she felt that squeeze all the way to places she should not be feeling it. Good God, what was wrong with her? She wanted to tell herself that it was because she hadn't had sex in so long that she was experiencing such a strong pull to Ellis, but that would be a lie. It was because of this man, Ellis Bishop. A man who was also wanted for murder and on the run for his life.

Every second she spent with him now, she found herself more and more attracted to him. And how stupid was that? Nothing could come of her attraction. Nothing good anyway.

As if he read her mind, he abruptly dropped her hand and cleared his throat, subtly shifting his body away from her.

Either he was repulsed by her—which she didn't think he was—or he knew that getting involved with her at all was stupid. He was right too. There would be no sidelong looks or kissing or anything.

Still, she couldn't help fantasizing what it would be like to kiss him. Maybe more than kiss him.

Her anxiety ratcheted up even higher as she wrapped her arms around herself. Just because she was scared of the future and completely off-balance didn't mean kissing this man senseless was a good thing. "So what now? What can I do to help?"

"We've had a long day. After seeing this I've got to make a couple phone calls, but you need to get some sleep."

"I want to help."

"You have helped. You went above and beyond anything you needed to do. What you did today was really brave." He looked her in the face then, those pale blue eyes of his mesmerizing. "Thank you. I don't deserve what you did."

"I don't know about that," she whispered. "I'm guessing you risked your life every day for a really long time. You didn't deserve to have the people who were supposed to have your back turn on you."

Instead of responding, he dropped his gaze to her mouth for what felt like the tenth time. Whenever his gaze strayed there, he looked at her as if all he could think about was plundering her mouth. And she would let him.

Even with her Frito breath, she still wanted to kiss him. But he looked away, focusing on the screen as the two men broke into her house.

She should have been focusing on that as well. Clearing her throat, she tried to get her stupid hormones under control. Ellis was being smart now, and she needed to take a page out of his playbook.

Pushing her chair back, she decided she didn't want to see some strangers traipsing through her house anyway. If Ellis didn't need her now, she figured it was much smarter for both of them if she put some distance between them. "I'm going to take a quick shower."

He nodded, not looking in her direction.

Feeling oddly bereft, she hurried from the room. She needed to take a very cold shower. Or she just needed to masturbate and get whatever this thing was out of her system.

CHAPTER THIRTEEN

Kyle Bird stepped into the dimly lit diner, pushing back his annoyance. No, his rage. He should be home in bed, not at the beck and call of Vitaly Rodin.

A dark-haired young man in his mid-twenties wearing jeans and a hoodie that most definitely concealed a pistol stepped out from behind the countertop. No one was in here at three o'clock in the morning so it was a good place to meet. But he didn't like being called out of bed without being told why.

"This way." The man motioned toward the swinging door that led into the kitchen.

Vitaly owned this place and used it as a front for some of his dirty deeds. Under normal circumstances Kyle wouldn't have met with the criminal in the middle of the night. But he had something on Vitaly—proof of murder. Kyle was untouchable right now and he planned to stay that way.

"What am I doing here?" he growled as he stepped into the nearly empty kitchen.

Vitaly stood next to a clean stainless-steel countertop. The diner had closed hours ago, and despite this place being in a low-rent part of town with questionable customers, the kitchen itself was immaculate.

Vitaly still didn't touch anything as he stood there in his three-piece, custom-made, thousand-dollar suit as if he was too good to meet with Kyle or be here at all. Please, the man was a criminal in nice clothes, but it didn't hide what he was.

Kyle's jaw tightened. "Well?"

The other man's ice-blue eyes narrowed slightly. "My stepdaughter has been taken." Usually his accent was barely discernible but tonight it was thicker.

He blinked, his anger fading into surprise. "What? When? How?"

The other man watched him carefully. "You don't know of this?"

"No. Who took her, and what do they want?" Kyle stepped farther into the kitchen and leaned against one of the countertops before pulling out a cigarette. It was impossible to smoke anywhere anymore but Vitaly didn't say anything as he lit up. Probably because the other man smoked as well.

"I don't *know* who took her. But one of my biggest accounts in the Caymans under her name was closed as well." A muscle ticked in his jaw, his eyes filled with rage.

He blinked as he took a drag on his cigarette. "Holy shit. Someone closed the account? Or they transferred funds?"

"Closed it in person. I have a video from the bank." Another tightening of his jaw. "It appears to be my stepdaughter."

Kyle didn't know what to say to that. As far as he knew, Arianna Stavish had no idea about her stepfather's business. Yet she'd closed an account Vitaly had set up in her name? He took another drag, waiting for the man to continue.

Vitaly finally spoke again. "I received a text message from a burner phone with her picture and a simple note telling me that she has been taken and that someone has my money. One of my guys has managed to get security feeds from inside the bank, outside it, and at a private airport, and she was definitely forced to close the account."

Kyle let out a low whistle. This was...not good. Vitaly's stepdaughter had been kidnapped and forced to close accounts she hadn't even known existed. Considering Kyle had helped the other man cover his tracks, he didn't like any of this. The only way he continued to get paid was if Vitaly had income moving in, and as long as he stayed alive and out of prison. And since Kyle had two divorces under his belt and owed a shitload of alimony and child support, he didn't mind helping Vitaly in the least.

This was a young man's game and he was ready to get out and retire. Just as soon as he got his final payday. "What do you want me to do?"

"I want you to use your resources and find out who took her," Vitaly growled, his eyes shards of ice now.

Kyle knew the other man didn't care about his stepdaughter, not truly. The only thing that mattered to Vitaly was money. He'd cared about his son, and maybe his dead wife, but Arianna was nothing to him as far as Kyle knew. She wasn't his blood, and blood was the only thing that seemed to matter to him. "I'll look into it. You sure she's not involved somehow?"

Vitaly snorted as if the thought was ridiculous. "Arianna? No. She's a naïve little fool." He shrugged. "But no one takes what's mine. I want my money back."

There it was. Vitaly's greed. Kyle nodded even though he hated taking orders from Vitaly. But that was just the way the world worked. Five years ago, Kyle had been deep in debt and close to losing his house to foreclosure when Vitaly had approached him with a deal. So Kyle looked the other way sometimes and Vitaly had started climbing the ladder in his criminal organization.

It had been a win-win for both of them. Kyle had given Vitaly good intel so that he avoided arrest and made Vitaly's boss, Leonid Berezin, look inept. It had started sowing the seeds so that Berezin would eventually fall—and Vitaly wanted to take his place when he did.

Over the last five years Vitaly had slowly been shifting people around to suit his need, making allies, and now he was set to take over the East Coast organization and start distributing a new type of drug into Florida. If all went well, he planned to take over certain channels on the eastern coast completely and make himself into a king.

Which meant Kyle was going to get paid handsomely. And then he was going to retire and disappear because he had no doubt that one day Vitaly was going to come for him as well, for knowing too much. He didn't like that Kyle had evidence of him murdering an undercover federal agent. Too bad for Vitaly. It was his safety net. And Vitaly never should have killed Carter in the first place. That had never been supposed to happen. But it had, so Kyle had made the best of a bad situation.

Kyle put out his cigarette under his foot, leaving the ash and butt on the floor. "I need those videos." He could get them with his resources, but he didn't want to use official channels for this. Not yet anyway, and not unless it was necessary. But he wanted to see if he could figure out who had taken Arianna—if it had been Ellis Bishop.

"I'll send them. But the man's face is hidden the entire time. I don't know if it's a crew or just one man."

"Noted. I'll check out her house too."

"No need. I've already sent people over there. She's definitely been taken but I don't want this reported. I want to keep it quiet. No one will know that someone took her. I cannot afford any distractions right now."

Meaning Vitaly couldn't afford to look weak, not when he was gearing up to take out Berezin.

"I'll be in touch."

Vitaly simply nodded, his expression a carefully controlled mask as Kyle left. Kyle hadn't asked, but he was curious who Vitaly had sent over to the girl's house. He knew Vitaly had other agents on his payroll but he didn't know who all of them were.

And that was the kind of information he could use. Maybe he would stop by the girl's house anyway. But first he needed to look at those videos and put out feelers—to see who would be stupid enough to cross Vitaly Rodin.

CHAPTER FOURTEEN

Ellis sat back in his chair as he heard the guest bedroom door across the hall quietly shut. He couldn't believe he was so stupid. Unfortunately, he couldn't keep his distance from Arianna. Not now. And not just because they were staying under the same roof.

Because he wanted her with the desperation of a starving man.

Rubbing both hands over his face, he groaned at his own stupidity. He was just sleep deprived, that was all. He had to stop this growing obsession he had with her.

But he couldn't. Because if this had been any other circumstance, he would have already asked her out on a date. Hell, they'd have probably already been in bed together. And he knew himself well enough that once they slept together, he wasn't letting her go. She was a diamond and he wanted to keep her, to hide her away from the shitty world and keep her safe. It stunned him that no one had scooped her up yet. Miami's loss was going to be his gain.

No. He had to stop thinking like that. Because they had no future. He was on the run for his life, and getting his life back was the only thing he should be focused on—not the stepdaughter of the man who'd killed his best friend.

Pulling out one of his burners, he called Lizzy.

She picked up on the third ring. "Living the nerd life," she said cheerfully.

He blinked at her odd greeting. "Is that how you answer the phone now?" he asked dryly.

She snorted. "I wasn't sure who was calling. How are you?"

"Still alive." And that was something.

"Well I've been digging into your former boss, and Bird definitely has some accounts tucked away. Tucked away *deep*. I technically can't link them to him, that's how good these accounts are. But they're his and I'm sure with more work I'll be able to somehow link him to the accounts. I just don't know what kind of traps he might have set up and I don't want him getting an alert that someone is looking into him."

"Thank you." It was a whole lot more than he'd had yesterday. He'd known that his former boss was dirty but he hadn't been able to find anything concrete on him.

Bird had worked undercover for a decade before taking a more senior role in the office and the man was sharp. Unlucky in love, considering his divorces—and his alimony was probably part of the reason he'd turned traitor—but he was good at getting the job done. Regardless of the reason Bird had turned, Ellis was going to make sure that traitor paid. That man had been a friend to both Ellis and Carter. There was a special place in hell for people who could turn on their friends like that.

"Oh, there's more. I have a treasure trove for you. Nothing we can take to the Feds yet, but it looks as if one of Bird's burner phones has been seeing a lot of action lately. He's been communicating a lot with one of Vitaly's underlings. It's not proof of anything—and I came by the information of his burner illegally—but I find it interesting. And he just got a call barely an hour ago."

"I'm not surprised. Knowing what I know now, he's been working with Vitaly for years. So many things make more sense now. Like busts that ended up going sideways because Vitaly's guys got tipped off. I know where the leak was coming from." He tightened his hand around the phone, imagining how good it would feel to punch Bird right in his throat. Then keep punching.

"Well, the guy does have a couple divorces and a lot of debt. Though recently he's cleared out most of his debt. He hasn't bought anything flashy, but he's paid off one of his kids' college loans too. Or someone has, because it hasn't come directly from one of his accounts."

"It's always about money," Ellis muttered. "Though I think this is about more than money for Vitaly. He's looking to take out his boss." Leonid Berezin was a tough bastard, but over the last few years he'd lost a lot of his inner circle to DEA busts and murders by rivals. Vitaly had been next on their list to take down—or so Ellis thought. God, he was such a fool.

"Yeah, I looked over the stuff you sent me and I agree," Lizzy said. "Vitaly has been playing the long game with his boss and it's so subtle that unless you know about the people in the DEA Vitaly is paying off, I'm not surprised Berezin hasn't figured it out."

"Yep. He's playing the long game for sure." Ellis cleared his throat. "Look, I've got to tell you something."

He quickly ran down everything that had happened in the last twenty-four hours, not leaving anything out.

"Holy shit," Lizzy said as he ended.

"Yeah, it's a lot. Arianna is currently getting some sleep but soon enough we're going to have to deal with all this. I'll know my next move once I talk to Vitaly and I see how he responds to my demands, but I wanted you to be aware of her involvement."

"She's taking quite a risk."

"I know. And I need to find out why Vitaly set those accounts up in her name. Preferably before I meet with him. I think I know why, but I'd like some confirmation. And since there are more accounts, I need to trace all that activity back to him. I need to be able to prove that it wasn't her who opened any of them. I don't want any of this falling back on her."

"I'll work on that too. Maybe you'll get lucky and Berezin will just kill Vitaly and your former boss."

He snorted softly. "Yeah, well, that would be great, but I need Bird and Vitaly in jail for killing Carter. And I need my name cleared." That was, if he ever wanted to live a normal life again—which he did. He could go on the run and start over somewhere but that was his last option, and the longer he was around Arianna the more he realized that he really didn't want to run. There was a spark of something true between them. More than a spark, if he was being honest, and he wanted the chance to explore it, to see if it was as genuine as he thought it was. "I just wish I had that video," he muttered. If he still had it, none of this would have ever happened. Vitaly would be in prison—probably dead.

"What video?"

He frowned. "The video of Vitaly killing Carter." What did she think he was talking about?

Lizzy sucked in a sharp breath. "What. The. Hell."

"I told you about it."

"No you didn't tell me. Are you kidding me? What happened to it?"

God, he was so damn sleep deprived. He swore he'd told her about it. "I took the video on my cell phone, and when I met up with Kyle he took the phone from me. I'd actually emailed a copy to myself before that meetup, but by the time I was able to get to a computer, he'd already deleted it. He'd wiped my entire account clean." He cursed inwardly at that, trying not to play the "what if" game in his mind. What if he had just been faster? Carter would still be alive. What if he hadn't trusted the wrong person? Carter would still be alive. *Ugh.*

"Holy shit, you should have told me this before. I need all information on what email accounts you used. Which one you sent it to and what account it came from."

"He's wiped it." Ellis had already thought of all the ways he could retrieve that video and it was impossible. Lizzy might be a great hacker but she couldn't do the impossible.

"Nothing is ever truly deleted on the web. *Nothing.* It is very hard to do. Not to mention..." She paused and he heard soft tapping in the background. "There is no way Bird didn't make copies for himself."

"Yeah, I figured he's got a couple copies stashed somewhere as backup for himself." It would be insurance against Vitaly so that Bird stayed untouchable. "But that does me no good."

"Oh, this is good news, my man." She made a cackling sound and he could practically see her rubbing her hands together with glee. "I'm going to dig even deeper into him. He would keep copies in random secure locations if he's smart. A bank or deposit box somewhere. He'll have an online backup and a hard copy, I guarantee it. I'm going to find out if he's opened any physical accounts recently and see what of his I can hack."

"He'd be smarter than that. He wouldn't want Vitaly to have the same thought process as you."

"I'm smarter than this fool. I'm going to find any stashes he's got and we're going to take him down."

He wished it were that easy, but against his better judgment he allowed hope to bloom inside him anyway. Given his circumstances, he knew it was stupid, but the hope was there, burrowing its way deep inside him. "Thank you, Lizzy. Seriously."

He was starting to feel hopeful for the first time in months. It was so real, so brutal, he was afraid to hold on to it. He was so afraid to hope at all in case it came crashing down around him. Because then he would lose everything, and that included Arianna. Not that he had her, but some part of him wanted a chance with her even if it was a fairy-tale hope.

"I've got another favor to ask you. I need to set up a place to meet with Vitaly if the next stage of my plan goes the way I think it will. I'm going to need something to record that meeting."

"I'll get back to you." She disconnected before he could respond, but he wasn't surprised. He'd heard the fast typing across her keyboard and knew she'd be busting her ass for him right now.

"Who is Lizzy?" Arianna stepped into the room, silent as a wraith.

Surprised, he schooled his expression and turned around in his chair to face her. "No one."

She had on gray yoga pants and a T-shirt that had an apple on it and said *Teacher of tiny humans* on it. She'd pulled her damp hair back into a ponytail and was watching him, eyebrows raised. "Sounds like someone."

Lizzy was helping him out, and despite her connections, he did *not* want her getting tangled up in any of this. He trusted Arianna, but it was all about plausible deniability. If she didn't know Lizzy's name, she couldn't tell anyone about it. "Just forget you heard that name."

She leaned against the doorframe, her body language anything but casual. "Are you involved with her?"

He let out a startled laugh. "No. Never. And her husband would shoot anyone who made a move on her." Not technically true, but Porter was obsessed and protective of his wife so...maybe it was a little true.

Arianna's shoulders relaxed slightly.

And he really wished he didn't notice that, wished she didn't care. But he liked that she cared whether or not he was involved with anyone. Because he was damn glad there was no one in her life.

"I know what you said before, but do you need help with anything?"

He rubbed his hands over his face and shook his head. "No, but thank you."

"You need food and sleep," she said quietly, not moving from the doorway. "And I know that you're a grown man, but seriously, you look exhausted. How much harder can you push yourself tonight?"

Something warm spread across his chest and he couldn't believe he'd ever thought this sweet woman was a criminal like her stepfather. "I know." He stood, stretching. "I'm going to take a quick shower."

"Good. When you get out, you're also going to eat. I saw some food in the fridge so I'm going to whip something up for us."

"You don't have to do that."

"I know, but I'm hungry too. And you eat like a twelve-year-old boy. The only things I've seen you eat are chips and Pop-Tarts. And not even the good kind of chips."

He lifted a shoulder, fighting a smile at her bossy tone. He wondered if this was what she sounded like when she was teaching. If so, it was beyond hot.

Her gaze lingered on his mouth for a moment before she turned away from him—and then he stared at her ass as she headed out, telling him she'd be in the kitchen.

He was not going to think about how oddly domesticated things felt right now. They were here for one reason only. But that didn't mean he didn't like being with her. He liked her company even though he hated that she was involved in all of this.

What if he had never seen those accounts? He wanted to know what her stepfather had planned to do with them long term and how his movements would have affected her.

No matter what, he was going to make sure Arianna came out the other side of this okay. Even if *he* didn't, she damn sure would.

CHAPTER FIFTEEN

"Thank you for cooking dinner," Ellis said as he picked up his plate and took it to the sink.

Arianna snorted slightly. "It's four in the morning. I think this is considered an early breakfast."

He paused before turning on the faucet. "My time frame is messed up. I thought it was still Friday night."

She could understand that. They'd had an insane day yesterday, taking a yacht down to the islands then getting on multiple private planes, and now they were back in Miami. Her sense of time was screwed up too because normally she'd be fast asleep at four in the morning. Curled up and dreaming about coffee. Now? She was edgy, and even though she was tired, she couldn't seem to turn her brain off.

She also couldn't help but notice Ellis had that freshly showered scent, and she liked whatever it was he was using. Very likely the Irish Spring soap from the bathroom. He was using one bar of soap and some off-brand shampoo that probably cost less than a dollar. And he smelled delicious.

"Omelets are easy, and you had everything." She stood and went to pick up her own plate but he plucked it from her hands.

"You cooked. I'll do the dishes."

She laughed lightly and realized she could probably sleep if she lay down. "I think since you originally kidnapped me, you get to do the dishes for all time."

He laughed again, a deep sound that rolled through her. It sent tingles of awareness and warmth spiraling throughout her in a slow, sensuous wave. He had a great laugh and he didn't do it enough. Of course she understood why but still, she wanted to hear more of it.

"I'm probably going to head upstairs and get some sleep." She knew he had people looking into things for him and would likely stay up and work more, even if he should be sleeping. The man had been working around the clock—because obviously he wanted to clear his name. But he wasn't a robot, and at a certain point he would end up burning out.

"I'm going to grab a few hours too. I'll sleep on the cot in the office."

She paused on her way out. "We shared a bed before. Feel free to sleep in the room with me." She was surprised by herself but screw it, she didn't care. Her life was a complete train wreck right now and his was far worse than hers. She wasn't going to outright invite him to do anything sexual, but there was no way she was letting him sleep on that sad little cot. It was too small for her, let alone him.

He shot her a surprised look over his shoulder.

"I'm just saying, the bed is big. You can sleep on top of the covers if it makes you feel better. Or I'll sleep on the cot," she added, hoping he didn't take her up on that.

He shook his head. "I would never let you sleep on that thing."

Yeah, after sitting on it before, she knew that it was lumpy and uncomfortable. She couldn't believe he'd been sleeping on it at all, especially given his big frame.

He looked at her again, something raw and hungry in his pale blue eyes. "I'll be upstairs in a little bit."

Her stomach flipped. She wasn't sure if he meant he was going to join her in the bedroom or not. And she hated that she cared. Really, really cared.

Right about now she wished she could call her sponsor and ask Sheila for advice but that was impossible. She'd allegedly been kidnapped, and in case her stepfather was monitoring anybody in her life, her sponsor was one of the first people he would look at.

No, she had to make decisions all on her own right now. Unfortunately, she was thinking very wicked thoughts about the sexy man doing dishes downstairs. And her brain and body were very much on the same page.

She wanted Ellis Bishop in her bed and not to sleep. Even with her past, she wasn't feeling anxious, but...turned on. Because Ellis wouldn't hurt her. Of that she was certain.

* * *

Arianna felt something warm and solid beneath her, and knew it was Ellis before she'd even opened her eyes. She was practically plastered on top of him, and using his chest—his very bare chest—as a pillow. And he was sur-prisingly comfortable. Though comfort was the last thing on her mind right now.

She breathed in his rich scent, enjoying his nearness and the way he had his arm wrapped tightly around her before she opened her eyes. Even with the curtains pulled over the window, she could see that it was still dark outside, so she couldn't have slept more than a couple hours.

She vaguely remembered him getting into the bed and she'd been drawn to all his heat and warmth. And okay, she'd just wanted to touch him. It should feel foreign to be curled up against him, to be seeking him out at all, but for some reason everything about this was right.

His breathing was steady, but she couldn't tell if he was asleep or not—and she wanted to know. When she looked up, she found herself looking into pale blue eyes filled with heat and hunger. All right, then. Very awake.

She swallowed hard, unable to tear her gaze away as he pinned her in place.

"You should be asleep," he whispered, sounding as if he'd swallowed gravel.

"So should you." She kept her palm on his chest, unable to move off him, unable to stop touching him. For some reason she was surprised he'd gotten into bed without a shirt, but she liked it. Okay, more like *loved* the sensation of skin to skin. The feel of his soft chest hair and sculpted pecs had her fingers itching to stroke all over him. He was all cut lines and sleek muscle and she was desperate to touch him everywhere.

Her nipples beaded tightly as she imagined stroking him everywhere and seeing his reaction. She should be nervous—and she kind of was, but in a good way. With Ellis, she knew on the most primal level that she was safe with him. Or at least her body was. Her heart was another matter. But in the here and now, she knew he could never, ever physically hurt her. Even when he'd thought she was a monster, he'd still been careful not to injure her.

He just watched her for a long moment and she felt his heart rate kick up underneath her fingers. The beat was wild and out of control, though to look at him she wouldn't have known, even with the unmistakable need in his eyes. Knowing that he was as affected as she was sent a rush of heat between her legs.

Her own heart rate increased as time seemed to stretch on forever between them. When he didn't say anything, she spread her palm against his chest and slowly moved down his muscled stomach. Lower and lower she went, inch by inch.

He sucked in a breath, all his muscles pulling taut, but he didn't make a move to stop her—and he easily could if he wanted. Ellis was so much bigger and stronger than her, something she was very much aware of. But she felt safe with him in a way she'd never felt safe before. Not with past boyfriends and not with her family. Being here with him now, she was free to do what she wanted until he told her to stop.

"Do you want me to stop?" Her voice was pitched as low as his had been. Some part of her was afraid to break this little bubble wrapped around them. They were in a quiet cocoon now that wouldn't last. She wanted to drag it out as long as possible, to pretend that this was their reality. That the outside world didn't really exist.

He shook his head, swallowing hard.

She kept going even as she kept her gaze pinned to his. She was tired of fighting her attraction to him and she knew that sooner or later—probably sooner—things were going to end between them.

Because they *had* to.

They were going to figure out how to clear his name and then what? He would go back to his life of under-cover work and she would go back to teaching. She was a realist, and a man like him was not looking to settle down. He was literally taking his life one day at a time right now because he was just trying to stay alive and out of jail. And he might not even clear his name. He could easily end up on the run for the rest of his life. Which was a depressing thought, so she wasn't going to waste another second. This might be the only night they had, and if he wanted this too, she was so in.

As she reached the waistband of his pants, her cheeks heated up at the feel of his thick cock jutting upward un-derneath his clothing. She was still watching his face and enjoying the way his cheeks darkened underneath his beard at her gentle touch. She'd never been this bold and she found that she loved every second of this. He made her want to be bold, to take charge—to be the woman she'd never gotten a chance to be before her life had changed.

Ellis groaned and closed his eyes as she ran her palm over his thick length.

And damn, he was big. His pants did absolutely nothing to hide that fact.

She clenched her thighs together as she imagined how incredible he would feel inside her, all thick and long and holy hell, he was killing her and they hadn't even done anything. Her imagination was going crazy and there was no way he could live up to it. Right?

"I should tell you to stop," he rasped out, trembling slightly.

But he didn't pull away, didn't try to move her hands. Nope, he rolled his hips up against her.

"Should I keep going?" she whispered. *Oh God, please, I don't want to stop.*

In response, he tightened his arm around her and basically lifted her until she was straddling him. *Oh, damn.* He didn't want her going anywhere, which was good. She simply couldn't walk away from him right now.

He wrapped his hands around her hips as she settled on top of him, his fingers flexing possessively. "Arianna." The way he growled out her name sent spirals of pleasure shooting through her.

Groaning, she shifted up onto her knees and felt his thick erection between her legs. *Oh wow. Yes, please.* She rose up slightly and then back down, grinding against him in a slow, sensuous rhythm. It didn't matter that they had layers of clothing between them, she felt the head of his cock rubbing against her clit with each stroke.

Watching her with heavy-lidded eyes, he tightened his fingers each time she ground down on him. Only the glow from a nearby streetlamp and other houses offered light through the drapes, but it was enough to see every flicker of expression on his handsome face.

She found that she liked being on top and felt somehow more powerful. She knew he could take over anytime he wanted, but she really enjoyed this position and the view.

She danced her fingers up over his rock-hard abs and chest, leaning forward so she could kiss him. Because his mouth was just begging for it. As she leaned down, he let out the sexiest sound ever and met her halfway, his mouth colliding with hers in a hungered frenzy.

Shifting position, she wrapped her legs around his waist as he lay there, in no hurry to change positions or do anything else other than explore his mouth. If this was the only time she got with him, she was going to squeeze every inch of pleasure out of it.

He explored right back, taking his time kissing her, slow and sweet even though she could feel the wild energy of him humming underneath her fingertips.

The sensation of his beard brushing over her chin and face sent more shivers of awareness buzzing through her. Above all, she liked this closeness, loved being completely sober and enjoying this. Because she would remember every second of this. Even two years ago she wouldn't have been ready for this closeness. Maybe because she hadn't met Ellis. With him, everything felt right. That in itself was scary.

She bit his bottom lip and he rolled his hips upward, his erection thick and heavy between them, even with their clothing still in the way.

At the moment she was glad they had clothes on because it would be so easy to give in to temptation and have sex with him right now. And maybe she would. But she needed to be a hundred percent sure. She could wait...a day.

She nearly snorted because the thought of even waiting twenty-four hours seemed too long.

But she forced her mind to slow down as she slid her hands around his back and dug her fingernails into him. His muscles tightened under her grip.

"I love your hands on me," he murmured against her mouth.

Oh, she loved it too. So, so much. Touching him was like touching raw power and she wanted to drown in him.

Slowly, he slid one of his big hands up under her T-shirt, his callused fingers skating over her back, just teasing her. As if he was completely satisfied with simply touching her there.

She wanted more but couldn't find her voice. So she rolled her hips against him again.

The friction of his thickness rubbing against her clit, even through the fabric, was incredibly erotic. More heat flooded between her thighs when he slid his hand up just a fraction higher.

She was actually turned on by him touching higher on her back. The whole thing should be ridiculous but oh God, she couldn't help but wonder if he was going to keep going higher. And she had to restrain herself from completely tugging her shirt off.

When he finally—finally!—slid his hand up her ribs and shifted around until he could cup her breasts, she practically sobbed into his mouth. Her nipples beaded tightly under his teases and her inner walls clenched around nothing as he tweaked the tight buds between his thumbs and forefingers. His touch was so damn gentle, yet she was about to combust. Maybe she really had been touch-starved.

Or maybe she was reacting this way because this was Ellis, a man she instinctively trusted with her body.

He groaned into her mouth as he fully cupped her breasts. "This is probably a mistake," he rasped out, his words jumbled against her mouth.

"So?" She didn't care if it was. He was a mistake she would make again and again. As long as she got to come. Because seriously, if they were doing this, she wanted orgasms. Lots of them. She had years to make up for.

He let out a short laugh, the rumble reverberating right through her.

Her nipples beaded even tighter as she continued grinding against him. God, she felt like a horny teenager, unable to get enough of him. He was addicting in a far different way than she'd ever experienced. This should be wrong on so many levels but everything about it felt right. Everything about *him* felt right. She'd been more honest with him about who she was than some of her friends, as if she knew him on a different level.

"Fuck," he growled against her mouth. "You're going to make me come in my pants." He sounded almost embarrassed by the fact but she didn't care.

The fact that he was as turned on as her sent another rush of heat between her legs. "Me too."

"Seriously?" Again it was like he'd swallowed gravel.

Shifting again so she straddled him completely, she continued rubbing herself over him. "You're teasing my clit...it feels so good."

"Keep riding me." That was a definite order, one she wanted to follow.

She lost herself in the sensation as he plundered her mouth once again. Faster and faster she rolled her hips until she surged into orgasm. "Ellis," she cried out as her climax surged through her.

It wasn't the most intense orgasm she'd ever had—it was barely taking the edge off—but she fell into it, savoring every second as the tension inside her body melted away with a pure rush of pleasure.

He buried his face against her neck and she knew he was coming as well as he shook against her, trembling and tightening his arms around her back as he thrust his cock against her over and over. Finally he stilled underneath her as he feathered little kisses against her neck.

She shivered at the contact, a smile playing against her lips. Breathing hard, she leaned back to look at him.

"I don't know if I should be embarrassed or not," he murmured, nipping her bottom lip between his teeth. "I don't think I've come in my pants since I was fourteen."

She laughed at his admission. "Well I've never come like that before." She usually needed a lot more stimulation, but she hadn't had sex in years. And before that? Not good sex. Not after— She shut that down, not letting her mind wander.

There was no room for that here in this bed and in this space with Ellis.

Right now there was only room for her and Ellis and the limited time they had together. She wasn't going to ruin anything by getting lost in her head.

To stop her thoughts from spinning away from her, she kissed him again.

CHAPTER SIXTEEN

"We need to head out and make the call." Ellis tightened his arm around Arianna as they lay in the bed. He had to make the "ransom" call to her stepfather and see if he could get Vitaly to meet with him. He should be ecstatic about finally getting to make a move on one of the men who'd ruined his life, but instead he hated that this took him one step further away from Arianna.

Inhaling her sweet scent, he stared up at the ceiling, desperately wishing they had met under different circumstances. He'd never railed against any higher being about life being unfair. Not until today. He'd had a good life until he'd gotten royally screwed—and now he was clawing his way back to that life, desperate to prove his innocence.

More than ever he wanted to get his life back, for reasons he was too afraid to hope for. But there was a spark of something so achingly real between him and Arianna. As insane as it sounded in his own head, he knew it was true. He had never met anyone like her and she'd gotten to him in a way he'd never experienced before.

"I know we have to get up." Her breath was warm against his chest as she lay curled up against him, still not moving.

In the alternate reality he imagined he'd met her in, he could see the two of them lying in a big bed like this together, watching a movie or making love before they both went off to work. Ellis would take great joy in waking her up in the mornings by eating her out. They might even get a dog from the shelter. Yeah, he could see that in his head easily.

Sighing against the spreading ache in his chest, he closed his eyes. "I need to shower before we head out."

She was silent, unmoving for a long moment. "Do you want company?"

He hadn't been ready to move at all until her softly spoken question. All the muscles in his body pulled taut as he shifted underneath her. He should tell her no, that what they'd just done was it, that they couldn't do anything else like that. Because coming with her had barely taken the edge off. He was still desperate for more of her.

"Yes," he managed to rasp out. Like she even needed to ask.

She pushed up slightly and brushed her lips against his, leaning into him.

He groaned into her soft kiss and started to tighten his grip around her, but she moved back out of his hold and slid off the bed. To his surprise, she started stripping, leaving her pajamas in her wake as she headed to the bathroom, and his heart skipped a beat.

Unable to move, he stared at her heart-shaped ass as she sauntered away from him. *Oh, damn.* He struggled to drag in a breath as he jumped from the bed and hurried after her. He'd follow that beautiful, naked ass anywhere. He'd follow *Arianna* anywhere.

"You have the best ass I've ever seen," he said as she turned the showerhead on.

Standing in the shower enclosure, she gave him a startled look over her shoulder. With her long hair falling against her back in waves, she let out a delighted little laugh. "Well I've only seen yours with pants covering it, but from what I can tell you've got a pretty nice one too."

That was when he realized he was still half dressed. Ah, hell. In bed he'd left his clothes on to keep a barrier between them, but now it was just ridiculous. He'd been so caught up in following her, he hadn't been paying attention to anything else, least of all his damn pants.

Before he could reach for the waistband, she stepped away from the jets and back to him where the curtain was still halfway pulled back. Slowly, sensuously, she ran her fingers along the edge of his jogging pants. As she did, he stared, taking in every inch of her, naked and gorgeous in front of him. Her light brown nipples were tight little buds against her bronze skin and it took all his restraint not to cup her breasts and lean down to suck on them.

He wanted to, but for now he was letting her set the pace. It felt important that she got to after having so much control stripped away by the situation he'd put her in before.

She shoved at his pants, and as they fell down his hips her eyes widened when she saw that he was commando.

She sucked in a sharp breath as she took in his size, and okay, a bit of pride swelled through him because it was clear she liked what she saw. He was thick and hard between his legs, and he felt bigger than he ever had. Because she was right in front of him, naked and gorgeous and touching him.

He stepped inside and tugged the shower curtain into place, enclosing them.

She let out a little yelp of surprise as he pulled her under the rushing water, but he turned so that he took the brunt of the jets. As she settled against him, her full breasts rubbing against his chest, for just a moment he could pretend that the outside world didn't exist. That he was really living in that alternate reality where they'd met in a bookstore or in a park, instead of him kidnapping her at gunpoint.

Reaching up, he gently cupped her face, struggling to find a way to convey all the feelings inside him. "I wish I'd met you under different circumstances," he murmured.

"Yeah, kidnapping me wasn't exactly a meet-cute." Her lips quirked up but he couldn't force himself to smile.

He wanted to remember everything about this moment with her, every single second. "I don't want you to go," he whispered.

That delicious curve of her lips fell. "Me neither."

They were both hurtling toward an ending to whatever this thing between them was. Soon, he was going to have to let her go. Until then... He kissed her, savoring the feel of her heavy breasts against his chest as he teased his tongue against hers. Yep, this alternate reality was amazing. She didn't have an evil stepfather and he wasn't wanted for murder.

He took his time kissing her as hot water splashed against his back, steam rising around them. She tasted sweet and perfect and he was already addicted to her.

When she arched against him, he slid a hand between their bodies and cupped her breasts, enjoying the fullness of them. He couldn't seem to get enough of her.

She whimpered as he teased her nipples in slow, little strokes. Her entire body trembled against him and he knew she needed more. He did too, but right now wasn't about him even if his cock was thick and heavy and so damn insistent between them.

He slid one of his hands lower until he was cupping her mound. She spread her legs immediately even though she let out a gasp of surprise when he teased her swollen folds.

When she'd been grinding on him earlier, it had felt wild and out of control and almost like they'd been teenagers.

Right now was different, more intense and sensual, and he needed to taste her.

Stepping forward, he moved her until her back was flush against the slick tile wall. She dug her fingers into his shoulders as he ate at her mouth. But her mouth wasn't enough. He needed more. With willpower he didn't know he had, he tore his mouth from hers and knelt down in front of her.

Breathing hard, she stared down at him with wide eyes. "What are you doing?"

"You shouldn't have to ask." He grinned up at her even as he gently took her ankle and lifted her leg over his shoulder.

She looked so innocent and almost shocked in that moment as she simply blinked down at him. There was no way a man had never gone down on her before. Was there? No, absolutely impossible. Men would be lining up to give her anything she wanted and worship at the altar of her curves and sweetness. He certainly wanted to.

"I've been fantasizing about this," he murmured as he leaned closer.

"Really?" Again, she sounded surprised and a little unsure of herself.

"Hell yeah." He didn't like that tiny bit of doubt in her tone. She should never doubt anything when it came to herself. And if for some reason this was her first time with a guy going down on her? "Has anyone...ever gone down on you?"

Her cheeks flamed now as she watched him, simply shaking her head.

Yep, men in Miami really were stupid. And he was definitely going to make sure this was perfect for her. Leaning forward he gently flicked his tongue against her swollen clit. It was impossible not to since it was peeking out from her pink lips, just begging for his tongue.

"Oh, God." She speared her fingers into his hair as he slowly, teasingly started sucking on her clit.

This was heaven. Teasing along her slick folds with his finger, he barely pushed inside her as he added more pressure to her clit. Using the little moans and gasps she made, he learned what she liked and didn't like. Though to be fair, she seemed to like everything, if the way she kept rolling her hips against his face and digging her fingers into his head was any indication.

He didn't have nearly enough time with her. Though nothing would ever be enough. He wanted everything from her. All her kisses, her sexy looks...everything.

He wanted to go back in time and make that alternate reality theirs. To experience the joy of waking up to her in her little house or his. Not this safe house where they were on borrowed time. He shoved out those thoughts and the accompanying stab of anger with them.

As he slid a finger fully inside her, she let out the sweetest sounding moan.

He rolled his hips into nothing in response. Just the sound of her cry of pleasure had him desperate for release, desperate to fill her up.

But that was too bad.

He would get himself off later, but for now he felt manic with the need to bring her to release. She deserved as many orgasms as she could take.

Slowly, he slid another finger inside her and she let out another strangled moan. "Ellis."

All his muscles pulled taut at the sound of his name on her lips. The water pounded down around them and even though he wished this could last forever, he needed her to come.

Adding more pressure to her clit, he started thrusting his fingers in and out of her in a slow rhythm. Her inner walls started tightening around him, but she wasn't there yet.

He wished he had more hands or another mouth so he could kiss and pleasure her everywhere at the same time. "Touch your breasts," he ordered against her.

One hand left his head and he looked up to see her following his order—and that in itself was hot as fuck—slowly teasing one nipple between her thumb and forefinger.

God, the sight of her like that—her hair wet and slick against her face, water rolling down her body as she touched herself—and he was about to come like he had no experience.

It was a miracle he didn't. But not again. He had more control than that. He hoped. Renewing his efforts against her clit, he found a steady rhythm, teasing her until he felt her inner walls grow tighter and tighter, milking his fingers.

And when he added a third finger, she jerked wildly against him and surged into orgasm. This climax was much harder than the one from before, her entire body trembling as he continued teasing her until she collapsed against the wall, her hands falling to her sides. He felt barbaric but a sharp possessiveness swept through him that he'd just given her this. More than just possessive, he felt territorial. He wanted everyone in Miami to know she was off-limits—that she was his.

"No more," she whispered.

He could do this all day but he stood and cupped her face with both hands, wishing again he had the right words to tell her what she meant to him. They were stuck somewhere in his brain, refusing to get out.

Wordlessly, he bent his head and took her mouth with his, and when he kissed her it felt like coming home. She was everything he'd never realized he'd been missing. As she flicked her tongue against his, he jerked in surprise as she wrapped her fingers around his erection.

Oh yeah.

Smiling in pleasure against his mouth, she started stroking him as they kissed, and for the second time that morning, he came, this time all over her stomach and breasts.

Long and hard, his climax seemed to go on forever, and feeling like a caveman, he rubbed himself into her skin, wanting to imprint himself on her everywhere.

He wanted her to remember him, because when this ended, he was never going to forget her.

CHAPTER SEVENTEEN

Arianna's heart was an erratic beat as she waited for Ellis to make the necessary phone call.

"You don't have to listen to this," he said as they sat in the truck outside the random warehouse he'd chosen. From their position they could see if anyone approached and the building gave them a decent amount of cover. And it had no security cameras.

He'd given Arianna a wig and a ball cap to wear as well as oversized sunglasses, so she'd sat in the front seat with him, not worried about any CCTV cameras capturing their images. Ellis seemed to understand exactly how facial recognition software programs worked and apparently they weren't as cool as she'd always thought. There was a high error rate, and even changing certain facial things or just covering them messed up the software. And with her disguise she was nearly unrecognizable. "No, I want to listen. I know in my heart that he set up those accounts, but I want to hear him say it." She needed to.

Jaw tight, Ellis simply nodded and made the call.

She kept her hands folded tightly in her lap, sitting quietly as he turned on the voice synthesizer.

"Who is this?" Her stepfather's voice came through the line loud and clear, his words clipped and concise.

There was the faintest hint of an accent but it was barely discernible.

Her stomach tightened at hearing him on the other end. She knew that all of this was real but still, the bizarreness of it all overwhelmed her. Just a few days ago she'd been an elementary school teacher living in ignorant bliss. Now? She knew her stepfather was a monster.

"I texted you yesterday. If you ever want to see your daughter again, you'll meet with me today. We have some things to discuss."

Her stepfather made a scoffing sound. "You can keep my stepdaughter. I want my money."

Even though she'd expected Vitaly to push back against a kidnapper, for some reason she had *not* expected that. She hadn't expected him to dismiss her so easily and quickly.

Turning away, she looked out the passenger window as Ellis continued the call. His voice sounded normal to her, but she knew the app he was using would mask who he was. "I find it hard to believe you don't care about her."

Vitaly snorted. "She's not my blood. And you know what, keep the money," Vitaly spat, his voice actually trembling with his rage.

That brought her head back around. Eyes wide, she looked at Ellis but all his focus was on the phone as he frowned in confusion. "You don't want your money back?"

"Oh, I want it. And I will get it. So if I were you, I would run far and fast. Wherever you go, it won't be far enough. No one takes from me and..." He cleared his throat as if remembering himself. "Enjoy it while you have it." The phone went dead.

Swearing, Ellis took the battery out then tossed the pieces out the window.

She had the most absurd thought that he shouldn't be littering. "He doesn't care about the money?" she asked even though it was obvious because Vitaly had just said so. "Maybe this is just a ploy."

Ellis looked at her as he tapped his finger against the center console and she could see he was working something through in his mind. "Shit."

"What?"

"I don't think he was bluffing. And if he doesn't want the money, it's because he's making his move against Berezin." He tightened his jaw again, which seemed to be typical when he was frustrated.

"His move?"

"He's going to kill Berezin or have someone else do it. He's making his play to take over the East Coast operations and he's probably doing it today or tomorrow. It's the only thing that makes sense." He let out a savage curse and slammed his hand against the steering wheel.

That ball of worry in her stomach tightened even more. For years she'd suspected that Vitaly's business wasn't exactly on the up and up, but she'd never imagined anything like this. Nothing with guns or drugs, especially considering how Max had died. "So what does this mean?"

He scrubbed a hand over his face, tension etched into every line. "It means I have to find another way to get close to him. This was a long shot anyway."

Maybe, maybe not. It was clear that Ellis had definitely been banking on this helping him out. She hated the defeat in his eyes that he was trying to hide. "Is there anything I can do?"

"I need to get you into police custody." Even as she made a face at the word police, he shook his head. "Or federal custody. I'm not saying witness protection or anything, but... We need to come up with a plan for you to be found as a kidnap victim. It's the only way your stepfather will let this go as far as you're concerned."

Yeah, she knew that and was trying not to think too hard about it. "What about you?"

"He'll still be hunting for me, but he won't find anything. And soon he'll have bigger problems if he's taking out Berezin. Look, my friend Lizzy—whose name you still need to forget—might know someone. Actually...I might know someone else I can call." He tightened his jaw again and though he was looking at her she realized he wasn't seeing her at all. She could practically see the wheels in his head turning as he came to a decision. Wordlessly he looked away from her and started the engine.

"Ah, are you going to fill me in on whatever you just decided?" she asked.

"Not yet. I'm still thinking this over in my head. I want to make sure you're picked up by someone I trust. Someone completely untouchable. It needs to happen quietly because your stepfather will want to talk to you afterward. And you have to look completely innocent. It's the only way you walk away from this."

Unfortunately he was right. If Vitaly thought she might be involved with this and not just a victim, he would kill her. At this point she had no doubt. "I can't believe he just dismissed me so easily," she whispered. "I don't understand what my mother ever saw in him." Okay, that was a lie—Vitaly had provided a nice lifestyle for her mother and it was something her mama had desperately needed, to feel...worthy and loved.

Reaching out, Ellis took her hand in his, bringing her knuckles up to his mouth. So very gently, he brushed his lips against her skin. "I'm sorry. Truly I am. I thought he would want you and the money back."

"We never had a warm and fuzzy relationship, but I think he loved my mother. Or...he loved the son she gave him. I know he loved my half-brother. And Max—sweet Maximus—adored me." She let out a tired sigh. "We adored each other, so maybe Vitaly just...put up with me, I guess. I can't believe he didn't even try to fight for me."

Ellis was silent as he kissed her hand again and put the truck into drive. There was nothing more to say anyway as they headed back to the safe house. He'd told her that he hadn't wanted to make the call anywhere near there in case Vitaly had been working with the DEA and had tracking technology. He wasn't sure what kind of technology Vitaly had for tracing a call or anything else.

Now time stretched out as she digested her stepfather's easy rejection and the reality that she and Ellis had to come up with something to make sure she looked like an innocent victim. If they didn't, she could never return to her life without the threat of Vitaly coming after her.

CHAPTER EIGHTEEN

Ellis ended the call and looked at Arianna, who was sitting on the kitchen countertop, her fingers wrapped tightly around the quartz on either side of her. "How do you feel about the plan?" he asked.

They'd figured out what they thought was a solid plan, even if he hated part of it. He was going to leave her abandoned in the back of an SUV. Then he was going to call in a tip to the local police. Lizzy's detective brother-in-law was going to be on standby and ready to swoop in and be the first one on scene. That way Arianna would get into police custody with someone he trusted and all of this would be on the record.

He did *not* want her in the hands of her stepfather now. How about never. But definitely not now when it was pretty clear to him at least that Vitaly was soon going to be making a move on Berezin. Things were going to get violent and bloody. And it was pretty clear she was disposable to him.

"If you trust this detective, then I will too." She pushed off the kitchen counter and reached for him as if it was the most natural thing in the world.

Humbled that she trusted him so much, he pulled her close, hugging her tight. She fit right against him, as if they'd been made for each other. "We'll go over every-thing tonight so it's all fresh in your mind. We'll make sure you have your cover story down."

Groaning, she buried her face against his chest. "I'm not worried about that. I mean I *am* worried, but I'm just really going to miss you." As she finished, she looked up at him, her expression so open and vulnerable. She wasn't hiding anything from him.

It was instinctive to hide his emotions, but there was no reason to deny that he was going to miss her too. No reason to deny anything at all. "I'm going to miss you too," he rasped out. Though that seemed far too passive a way to explain his feelings. He'd spent years hiding the real him, always pretending to be someone else. So even though it was foreign, he continued as he cupped her face. "If I'd met you under normal circumstances, I would have asked you out on a date. And if I'd been lucky enough to get your phone number, I wouldn't have waited to call you and set up that date."

There was a slight sheen of wetness in her green eyes as she looked at him. "I would have said yes," she whis-pered.

Something shifted deep inside him. He couldn't stand this. Could not stand knowing he was going to have to let her go. "I want to say more to you, but it's not fair. I don't know what's going to happen after tomorrow." Be-cause he wasn't sure he'd be able to clear his name or get his life back. So he couldn't make promises to her he wasn't sure he would keep. "You need to be safe."

She wrapped her arms tighter around him, her lush body pressing against his. "I know. So let's not waste any of this time together." There was a desperation in her voice that he felt in his bones.

"You're the kind of woman I would walk away from this job for." He felt as if he'd swallowed gravel as he rasped the words out. That was as close as he could get to telling her how he truly felt. He didn't want to lay anything else on her, because tomorrow they would have to separate and he had no idea when he would talk to her next. If he ever would. There was no guarantee he was coming out of any of this alive.

Her eyes widened slightly as she grabbed onto his shirt and tugged him toward her.

Leaning down, he covered her mouth with his, needing to taste her again. Grabbing her by the hips, he hoisted her up and barely made it to the living room. He wanted to make it upstairs and into the bedroom but that wasn't happening. Not with how desperate they both were.

He grabbed some of the pillows and blankets on the back of the couch and tossed them down in front of the fireplace for a makeshift bed.

She clutched onto him, a soft smile curving her lips as he sat her on the bundle of blankets. One lamp in the corner was more than enough light, illuminating everything he needed to see.

He couldn't even force his mouth to curve upward in a semblance of a smile. There was too much inside him right now. Too much he was trying to keep in check. Because this was saying goodbye, something he knew on every level. He didn't want to let her go, but tomorrow he would.

Now... Now was for them. Instead of focusing on what he was losing, he was going to soak up every single second he had with her. It wouldn't be enough, but it would have to last. He would take these memories and *make* them last.

And just pray to a God he wasn't sure he believed in that he came back to her. Because when this was over, he was walking away from the DEA. If he cleared his name.

No, there was no room for those kinds of thoughts right now.

"Tell me to stop and we stop," he murmured as he reached for the top of her pants and tugged them off. He couldn't believe his hands were shaking, but they were. He could shoot a target at a thousand yards in poor wind conditions. But this? It was almost too much.

"Okay. But I don't want to stop." The need sparking in her eyes mirrored exactly how he felt.

And as she bared herself to him, quickly stripping off her sweater, he sucked in a sharp breath.

His erection pressed against his zipper as he stared at her in her bra and panties. A pink and black sports bra held up her full breasts and a little scrap of lace just barely covered her mound.

He'd seen her in the shower, had touched and kissed her everywhere—had been lucky enough to taste her as she came. But seeing her in this state of undress was still like a punch to all of his senses.

"What?" Her voice was low and she started to wrap her arms around her middle.

No way. He never wanted Arianna to cover up in front of him, never wanted there to be any barriers between them. "Nothing. I was just admiring the view." He inwardly winced because he sounded stupid, but if the way her cheeks flushed was any indication, he'd said the right thing. The truth was almost always the right thing.

He crawled over her, until he had her caged in underneath him. Propped up on his elbows, he looked down at her.

"I..." He couldn't find any words that didn't sound pathetically short of anything he wanted to express, so he leaned down and covered her mouth with his.

Thankfully she didn't seem to need any words because she arched into him, rubbing her unfortunately still covered breasts over his chest. He needed to get undressed too, but he enjoyed the feel of her wrapped around him.

Desperate for more, he slid his hands under her sports bra, cupping her smooth, full breasts against his palm.

She moaned into his mouth as he teased her nipples, the sound of her pleasure going to his head.

He ordered himself to go slow even though his body was trembling with unparalleled need. She was literally his fantasy woman and he couldn't believe she was in his arms right now.

Especially not after what he'd done. He didn't deserve her but he was damn sure going to do everything in his power to get back to her once this mess was settled.

That knowledge hit him with a gut-punching force. He would do anything to get back to her. He wanted to clear his name, but more than anything he wanted a future with her.

As she slid one of her legs lower, her heels rubbing against his ass and then wrapping around his upper leg, he rolled his hips against her.

He needed her completely naked right now. Shifting slightly so that he could lift his weight off her, he quickly took off her sports bra.

Her breasts spilled out, full and heavy, and it took all his self-control not to bury his face against them. Not yet.

Her dark hair splayed everywhere around her as he shimmied down her body and grasped the edges of her black panties. It took mere seconds to drag them down her legs. She was smooth and soft and perfect. Her skin was a perfect bronze that seemed to glow in the dim light of the living room lamp. He wished he had something better for their first time like candles or…something romantic that she deserved. But he hoped a couple orgasms would make up for it. "I wish I could give you more than—"

"Stop." Sitting up, she grabbed at the bottom of his shirt and tugged upward. "No what-ifs or wishing. We have right now. And I'm grateful for this time with you.

As insane as it sounds, I am grateful I met you. I can't imagine my life without you in it."

Damn. He swallowed hard as that intangible thing in his chest shifted again, settling even deeper. Meeting her had changed everything.

Leaning forward, he pressed his forehead to hers. For just a moment, he swore he could see, so clearly, all the way into the far-flung future, a reality with her that he so desperately wanted, and it carved an ache in his chest. It was a dangerous thing to want something too badly. Experience told him it always got taken away. But he couldn't stop wanting her, couldn't stop this obsession running full speed with no way to stop it.

So he kissed her hard, falling back on top of her as she stretched out underneath him, all lithe and sensual woman. All his. Her hard nipples brushed against his chest as he plundered her mouth once again. He was fully addicted to her taste, completely addicted to her, and he didn't care.

She reached between their bodies and rubbed a hand over his thick erection.

Shuddering under her soft touch, he growled against her mouth. The feel of her touching him was too much right now. He was barely in control as it was, balancing on a tightrope of restraint that was about to snap at any moment.

He tore his mouth from hers and slowly began kissing down her body, memorizing every inch, every dip and curve, until he knelt between her legs.

He'd seen and tasted her in the shower, but this somehow felt different. Because he knew this was about more than just sex. This was about more than the physical. At least for him. No, he knew it was for her too. It was like there was this unspoken thing between them that connected them.

Dipping his head between her legs, he flicked his tongue against her slick folds and nearly lost his mind. She was so damn wet and he knew it was all for him.

That alone made him feel powerful in a way he'd never imagined. He loved that he turned her on like this, that she was soaked for him and him alone. Because he was completely rock-hard for her. No woman had ever affected him like this. He'd been doing undercover work for so long and had seen the shittiest people in the world. And monsters didn't always look scary on the outside. If anything, they blended in. And pretty women were a dime a dozen, but Arianna was beautiful on the inside too.

Inside and out, Arianna was this bright star he would do anything to protect.

She rolled her hips against his face with an increasing urgency so he dipped two fingers inside her. Her inner walls tightened around him with surprising force.

His cock kicked against his pants as he imagined sliding deep inside her. But she had to come first. He felt crazed with the need to make her climax against his face even as he imagined how incredible it would feel to have her wrapped around his cock.

"I want you in me now." The raw words were torn from her mouth and when he looked up the length of her body, there was a riot of emotions in her green eyes.

He wanted the same thing too. God, did he ever. And he knew this one time wouldn't be enough. Not tonight. Not ever.

Moving lightning fast, he ripped off his jeans and put on a condom. As he settled between her thighs, just letting the head of his cock tease against her slick folds, he groaned.

He softly nuzzled his nose against hers once as they watched each other, needing even more contact. Her breathing was erratic as she looked up at him, her fingers digging into his back.

"You set the pace," he whispered. He wanted everything about this to be perfect for her, and just being able to touch her and be inside her was all he needed.

She smiled before brushing her mouth over his and her sweet kiss quickly turned frantic. *Fuuucck.* He nearly lost it as she rolled her hips upward again—at the same time he thrust forward.

She sucked in a ragged breath. It was too much and not enough.

She was so tight around him, and before he could ask if she was okay, she grabbed onto his ass.

"Start moving." Her words were raw emotion and pure demand. And he loved it.

Arianna had never felt so full and wonderful in her life. And as Ellis started thrusting inside her, she let out a moan of pleasure. She'd been so worried, wondering if she could have normal sex again, and until right now she hadn't realized that the key wasn't just about the physical act. It was about who she was with. And her complete trust in Ellis made this special.

She would give anything to be able to stay with him but knew it wasn't possible. So at least they had tonight, at least they had the next few hours. Because one time wouldn't be enough. Not for her anyway.

As he thrust inside her, over and over, she met him stroke for stroke, power surging through her. When he was on top of her like this, she felt protected and safe, a completely foreign feeling she wanted to soak up.

She clutched onto his back, digging her fingers into his skin. She didn't have to worry about hurting him, not a man like Ellis.

When he reached between their bodies and teased her clit, she surged into orgasm. She hadn't been expecting it so quickly but the pressure on her sensitive bundle of nerves, combined with his thick erection filling her, set her off.

"Ellis," she cried out as she arched into him, holding on to him as if her life depended on it.

He growled out her name as he buried his face against her neck. She loved the way he said "Arianna," like a desperate prayer.

He came with her in long, hard strokes, his big body shuddering with the force of it.

It seemed to go on forever, until they were both trembling with the aftermath of their orgasms.

Breathing hard, she gently brushed some of the hair that had fallen across his forehead.

He smiled down at her with a lazy, sated expression. But there was nothing smug about it. He looked satisfied and happy.

A mirror of how she felt.

"We have to do that a couple more times before tomorrow," she murmured.

A darkness flickered in his gaze as if he didn't want to acknowledge that tomorrow would come, but he nodded. "Definitely. I'm not remotely done with you yet."

* * *

Time was slipping away far too fast, like water through her fingers. Arianna was desperate to slow the clock down, but the more she wanted it to, the faster it seemed to go.

The last few hours with Ellis had been incredible, even if it wasn't nearly enough time. She trailed her fingers up Ellis's bare chest, soothed by his steady heartbeat and solid presence. She thought about not telling him her deepest secret before they parted ways, but she wanted to.

Because he'd given her back a part of herself she thought had died. And she trusted him with this. "I want to tell you something personal about me. Something I don't think you found in your files."

He stiffened slightly under her but didn't stop rubbing her back.

Light was peeking in through the windows as the sun started to rise. Time, just slipping away right in front of her.

Throat tight, she said, "When I was in college, at the start of my senior year, I was assaulted... No. I was raped. It's hard to say the words sometimes, even now."

All his muscles had gone tight underneath her but she kept going. She stayed where she was, with her head on his shoulder and her hand on his chest as she curled into him. He wasn't going anywhere and she felt grounded where she was.

"We'd been friends. Or I thought we had been, because clearly we were not. But I'd had a couple drinks at a party—not too much, just enough that I knew I shouldn't drive. Instead of taking an Uber, he said he'd drive and I had no reason to say no. We'd hung out in the same social circle for years and he'd never given off a creepy vibe. I'm not going to give you all the details because they don't matter, but it was violent and it happened in my apartment. My roommate came home early and called the police as he ran. There was no doubt that he'd done it, though he tried to say I wanted it." She let out a bitter-sounding laugh with no humor even as anger bubbled up inside her. "As if I asked to have my head bashed into a wall so hard I needed stitches."

She pushed back all the fear and haziness that threatened to invade her as she talked about this. She hadn't talked about her attack in years, not since she'd told her sponsor everything.

"It would've gone to trial because his family is wealthy and he would have fought it. But he died in a very violent carjacking not long after. My mom had breast cancer at the time, and as you know, she and my brother died close together. All of that happened at the same time. It's when my drinking started spiraling out of control. I went from having too many at a college party but not being blitzed, to being completely out of control. I have no idea if I would have become an alcoholic if all of this hadn't happened. But I think I would have. Alcohol releases something in my brain, changes the way I act and think—it's my brain chemistry, I guess. And I swear I am getting to a point." She realized she'd balled her hand into a fist against his chest and made herself release it, to take a deep breath.

He remained quiet, listening intently as he continued to rub her back. Which she was grateful for because she needed to be able to talk, to get all this out at one time. Then she didn't want to talk about it again.

"Before you, I hadn't had sex in three years. After I joined AA, for those first six months, a couple times I woke up in some random guy's bed, hungover, having completely blacked out the night before. And before that...I never had sober sex after what he did. I was on the pill back then but I'm just grateful I never got an STD or worse."

Now she looked up to find him watching her with compassion in those blue eyes. It threatened to shred her last vestiges of control.

"I just wanted to tell you that being able to share last night—and this morning—with you, has meant everything to me. You mean a lot to me." Her words didn't seem like enough in the face of what they'd shared, because she wanted to convey to him exactly how much he'd given her. But she was afraid that if she did, she'd start blubbering all over him.

Thankfully he seemed to be the perfect man because he cupped her cheek and leaned forward to brush his lips against hers. "Thank you for sharing that with me. I'm so sorry you went through that."

She sidled closer to him as his grip on her tightened. The fact that he'd simply listened meant everything to her. For a moment she thought about telling him that she suspected Vitaly had ordered the killing of her rapist, but didn't want to talk about him anymore. She just wanted to be here in the moment with Ellis.

Sighing, she laid her head back on his chest, treasuring the quiet for as long as they had it. Walking away from him was going to carve a hole in her chest.

Still, she wouldn't have given up a moment of their time to spare herself the pain she was about to endure.

CHAPTER NINETEEN

"Arianna, you need to see this," Ellis called out from the living room.

She hurried in from the kitchen, wearing jeans and a fitted T-shirt with her college's logo on it. "What?"

In response he turned up the volume on the flat-screen television.

On-screen a woman with auburn hair and a serious expression spoke somberly. "Authorities have confirmed that Leonid Berezin was found murdered in his home. Someone set fire to it as well..."

Arianna's eyes widened as she looked over at him. "What does this mean?"

"Looks like Vitaly made his move and killed Berezin," he murmured.

Feeling ill, she sat on the edge of the couch as the woman kept speaking. Ellis had told her that this would likely happen. "Okay, well what does this mean for me and you?"

"It's actually better for you."

That felt weird, considering that Berezin was dead, but she was going to move past that. She hadn't known the man, but according to Ellis he'd been a violent psychopath. "Explain, please."

He turned the volume down but didn't sit. Instead he crossed his arms over his chest and looked a bit like a

caged tiger. His muscles flexed slightly with his movements. "Vitaly has now made his big move by killing Berezin, which means he's in a position to take over. Or
he's certain he is. From what I can tell he's been slowly
eliminating Berezin's men for years. Even though I think
he still needs that money—he'd been saving it for a reason—me kidnapping you and stealing the money moved
that timeline up. But I don't think he'd have killed Berezin unless he had a solid plan in place to begin with. And
I guarantee my former boss helped him. So our plan for
you stays the same. There's no need for any of that to
change."

She rubbed her hands up and down her bare arms.
"Okay, I guess."

He was in front of her in an instant, crouching down.
"Look, I wouldn't let you go with the detective if I didn't
trust him one hundred percent."

She and Ellis had come up with a plan where she
would be found in an abandoned SUV by one of his detective friends. Or acquaintances, she was a little unclear
on the relationship. Ellis wanted her in police custody so
there was a record of the kidnapping and because the police would be looking a lot closer at her—which meant
her stepfather wouldn't do anything to her. Vitaly
wouldn't want to bring any more heat than necessary on
himself. It was either that or she stayed in hiding with
Ellis, and that wasn't an option for too many reasons.

"I know you trust him. I just... My record with cops
isn't great." She'd told him that before, but she needed to
give him more details. "After I was raped, the cops who

arrived on scene were...assholes. It shattered something in me. Something I'd believed in before. And I know not all cops are like that. Trust me, I do. Some of my friends at work are married to cops, but...I still have a hard time with them."

His jaw clenched and he opened his mouth to say something but stopped.

"What?"

"I want to hunt them down and bash their faces in for breaking your trust. And I'm sorry if that scares you."

She gave him a ghost of a smile, touched at his need to defend her. The man had an honorable streak so wide it was incredible that anyone he worked with believed that he'd killed his partner. She'd known him not even a week and she knew what type of man he was. The kind who had your back no matter what. "Tell me more about this detective." He'd given her basics but she wanted more.

"Well to start, his former partner works for Red Stone Security, and the woman whose name I told you to forget...she knows Detective Duarte personally. And she's been helping us for no reason other than she is a good person. I would never, ever put you in harm's way. Duarte is happily married, fights to protect those weaker than him, and my sister says he's a good one. I trust her judgment more than most."

Arianna cupped his cheek with one hand as she pushed her fears back. "Okay. I trust you. I just don't want to leave you." He closed his eyes and leaned into her touch and that pretty much just melted her right then and there. "You better get out of this mess," she ordered.

His eyes snapped open. "I will. Whatever it takes."

She certainly hoped so because she didn't want to imagine a future without him.

He took her hands in his and stood. "Ready?"

She snorted softly and wrapped her arms around him. "No. But let's go."

* * *

Ellis drove slowly to the designated spot. They'd set all this up over the last few hours, and even though he knew this was the best way to get Arianna into the right hands, he hated that he was leaving her. "How are you doing back there?" he asked.

"I'm good." Arianna was in the back of the SUV, her hands bound in front of her.

As soon as he parked the fully wiped-down SUV, he was going to leave and call in a tip about a kidnapped woman. Duarte had already confirmed he would be on standby, ready to take the call when it came in. He was nearby and it would take him five minutes max to get to her. And Ellis wasn't leaving his hiding spot until she was safe with Duarte.

From there she would go in to make a statement and Ellis had no doubt that her stepfather would immediately come to see her. He also had no doubt that Vitaly would check the 911 call and see if he could get a match on Ellis's voice. A man like that would cover different angles.

Every step Ellis took mattered, because it affected Arianna's life.

This was the only way he could protect her. He wished he could just keep her with him, but the longer he did, the more questions would come out later. This gave her the best option of returning to her life as seamlessly as possible.

She was going to tell the police that some random guy had kidnapped her and demanded a ransom from her stepfather. She would leave out the details about the bank account and trip to Grand Cayman, but planned to talk to her stepfather about it privately later. She was going to tell Vitaly she didn't trust the cops with that information because she wasn't sure how it would look for her—and act confused about how an account like that was in her name.

She'd wanted to wear a wire in the hopes of getting her stepfather to admit something, but no way would Ellis let that happen. He couldn't risk Vitaly discovering a listening device because he wouldn't be there to protect her from that monster. Ellis had no doubt that Vitaly would kill her if he thought she'd betrayed him. As it was, Vitaly had no reason to hurt Arianna at all as long as he believed she had been a victim. He gained nothing from it.

And while Ellis hated the guy, he knew that Vitaly didn't go around killing random women or abusing them. He cared about making money above all but he wasn't a violent psychopath, not like his predecessor Berezin. No, he treated his employees better and paid them better. Which was probably why so many had stepped in to work for him as opposed to the now dead Berezin. Those old-school ways of ruling with fear and violence definitely had their place, but so did better pay and fair treatment. And Vitaly had capitalized on that.

"I'm going to be able to see the vehicle the whole time," he said again. They'd gone over this, but he wanted to keep reassuring her. "As soon as Duarte arrives, I'll leave."

"Okay. And as soon as I make my statement, I'm going to head to an AA meeting. I'll contact my stepfather but I'll make sure to stay in public places."

"Good. You sure you have my burner phone number memorized?" He had an extra burner he'd never used. Now he was going to use it as his emergency number for Arianna should she need him.

She recited the number, easing some of the tension inside him.

"We're here." His heart rate kicked up as he pulled into the Starbucks parking lot. It was a decent neighborhood and he wouldn't have to worry about anyone messing with the vehicle for the few minutes he left her alone. "I'm parking now. There are a few vehicles in the parking lot, but it's mostly empty. I'm going to get out like we discussed, and make the call. Countdown five minutes."

"Okay."

"Stick to the script. Don't deviate from anything. As long as you stick to it, the police will believe you and your stepfather will as well."

"I know what to do... Take care of yourself." Her voice was sad and she might as well have punched him in the face.

"You too." It took every ounce of self-control he had to walk away. With gloved hands, he took the keys out of the ignition and tucked them into his pocket even as he pulled out one of his burner phones.

"911, how may I help?" the operator asked.

"There's a tied-up woman in the back of a black SUV at the Starbucks on..." He gave the address, speaking clearly so the dispatcher would have all the information. "She's been kidnapped, but I'm letting her go."

"Sir, can you repeat—"

Ellis hung up. Then he took the battery out but kept walking.

As he moved across the parking lot to a vehicle his sister had dropped off for him, he slid into the front seat and called Lizzy on another burner, while watching the SUV. Even though they had a solid plan in place, it still felt wrong leaving her. Like he was abandoning her.

She picked up immediately. "I made the call," he said to her.

"Carlito knows what to do. He has a lot of questions— like a whole lot, and now I owe him some favors—but he knows what to do."

From his position, Ellis had a clear view of the SUV. He'd parked it next to a dumpster and there wasn't anyone else on the other side. "Good. How are we doing on that other thing?"

"I can't find any accounts that Bird has opened up. No safety deposit boxes, nothing. Which really makes sense. He's got a piece of property up in North Carolina that's buried pretty deep in various company names, but it's his. It's like fifty acres though, and nothing is built on it so...if he hid it there, I don't know how we'd find it. It'd be like looking for a needle in a stack of needles." She sounded as frustrated as he felt.

He glanced at the time. Duarte should be there by now. *What was going on?* He looked around the parking lot, but there was very little movement. And no sirens in the background. "I'm wondering if he's got it at the office. It'd make sense because no way would Vitaly try to sneak into a DEA office to retrieve it. It'd be suicidal."

"Yeah, I thought that too."

Ellis glanced at the clock. Too much time had passed. He didn't like this at all. "Carlito still isn't here. I'm gonna grab her."

"Just give him another minute. You know what Miami traffic is like."

Screw that. He'd started to get out of the car when a pickup truck parked behind the SUV. Ice flooded his veins as a man he recognized got out of it and strode toward the back of the SUV doors.

"Shit." Ellis yanked open his door.

"What is it?"

"One of her stepfather's men is there. He's getting her out of the back."

Lizzy let out a curse. "Vitaly might have someone monitoring 911 calls."

He'd thought of that, but Duarte should have been there. That should have been a nonissue. Heart in his throat, Ellis pulled out a weapon and shut the car door behind him.

CHAPTER TWENTY

Arianna tensed as the back door handle jiggled. This was it. She just hoped this detective was as trustworthy as Ellis seemed to think. No, he would be. She trusted in Ellis and wasn't going to let old fears crowd into her head and take over. At that moment she also had to ignore the ache in her chest at the realization that she had no idea when she would see him again—if ever.

Suddenly the door swung open, the early Sunday morning sunlight nearly blinding her. She winced, then gasped in surprise when she realized it was Otto, one of her stepfather's men. In his late forties, he had a salt and pepper mustache and was in good shape. Like her stepfather, he'd been born in the US, but he didn't have any accent.

He seemed relieved to see her as he reached for her. "Come on."

Stunned, she held out her tied hands when he reached for them. "What are you doing here? How did you find me? That man said he was calling the police!"

Otto reached into his back pocket and pulled out a knife. She almost winced away but suppressed the action as he cut her wrist bindings free.

"Come on." He wrapped an arm around her shoulders as he helped her out of the back of the SUV.

Oh God, what should she do? That detective should have been here by now. She could hear a police siren faintly in the background and shuffled her feet, glancing around the nearly empty Starbucks parking lot. "Where are the police? Should we wait for them?" She fought the swell of rising panic as they neared his vehicle. She couldn't leave with him.

"Arianna," he snapped out. "We need to go. Vitaly does not want you involved with the police. Trust me when I say this, you don't want to be on the news. Let's go!"

She wanted to argue with him but couldn't see a good way to do it. And when a woman with a toddler in the back seat pulled into the parking lot next to them, she shut her mouth. She had no idea if Otto would hurt random bystanders if she fought him. She didn't want to think so but she wasn't going to take the risk. The man worked for Vitaly which meant he had to be at least somewhat ruthless.

As she went with him to the nearby truck, she saw Ellis stalking their way. It was clear Otto didn't see him across the parking lot that connected to a grocery store chain. She shook her head at Ellis to warn him off and got into the passenger seat, completely ignoring him. She couldn't risk him getting into something with Otto and blowing his cover—or that woman and her child getting hurt. No way. She just couldn't do it, even if it meant facing her stepfather.

As Otto slid into the front seat beside her, he reached out and squeezed her hand. "I'm glad you're okay." He sounded like he actually meant it, which made her want to relax just a little. He was one of her stepfather's few employees that she actually liked. He was always nice to her—he often said she reminded him of his daughter. And she didn't think he was lying, considering his daughter worked across the country and was also an elementary school teacher.

"I don't understand why we aren't waiting for the police." She had to play this up for all she was worth, had to be confused and scared. The scared part wasn't hard either.

Sighing, he pulled out of his parking spot after glancing in the rearview mirror. "Vitaly has been worried sick over you. He's had us all over Miami trying to find a lead on who could have taken you."

She held back a snort at the lie. She wondered if Vitaly had even told Otto about the call from Ellis, about the missing money. She had no idea if Otto was high enough up the food chain to be privy to that sort of thing. He hadn't been on Ellis's board of information so maybe he wasn't. She hoped not.

"We've been listening to police scanners and when we heard a call about a kidnapped woman, I figured I would check it out since I was so close. I can't believe it's you." He shook his head, pure relief in his voice. So okay, maybe they really had been listening to the scanner. Which was bizarre.

"Why were you listening to a police scanner?" she asked, because she figured that was a very normal thing to ask. She knew that people actually could listen to police calls in some areas and that there were apps for that very thing. *Freaking apps.* But she also knew that a lot of police departments had taken steps to block people from listening in.

"Ask Vitaly when you see him."

"I'm not going to Orlando. I want to talk to the police and I want to go home." She resisted the urge to turn around, to see if Ellis had followed them.

"Your father's here."

She almost said stepfather but reined in the correction. "What do you mean?"

"I mean he's here in Miami."

She knew he had a home here, one he rarely used. It was in a gated neighborhood and luxurious. Nowhere near like his estate in Orlando, which was on two acres in the city, something nearly unheard of. "I just don't understand—"

"Look, I don't have any answers for you. I just know that he's been turning over every rock trying to find you. Do I need to call a doctor to meet us there?" he asked carefully. "Are you...injured?"

She blinked until she realized what he meant, then shook her head and looked away. It was clear she wasn't going to get any answers from Otto so she sat back against the leather seat and kept her mouth shut. Right about now she figured that staying silent was the best thing.

"Whoever did this to you is going to pay," Otto said, maybe mistaking her silence for sadness.

She simply shrugged and kept staring out the window. Yep, she was keeping her mouth shut. Better to say nothing than slip up and say something that could get her or Ellis killed.

Barely half an hour later Arianna walked on numb legs to Vitaly's office, Otto escorting her. She received a few sideways glances from random men who clearly worked for Vitaly, but she ignored them. Her wrists were bruised and scabbing in places, which should help sell her story more.

Ellis hated that she'd scuffed up her wrists but she'd convinced him it would look a lot more realistic to the police this way. Maybe if she'd been a different person, if she had different experiences, she wouldn't have felt the need to prove what she'd been through, but she did. And Vitaly was observant enough that he would notice the bruising.

Otto opened the door and quietly ushered her in before ducking back out.

Her stepfather was on his cell phone and nodded once at her as he quickly ended his call. There was no relief in his eyes to see her—which was very telling. If she'd held out any sort of hope that he cared at all about her, it died a sad death right then.

As he set his phone down, he hurried around his desk and came to her, gently taking her by the shoulders in his weird version of a hug. "Otto texted me. He said…you don't need to see a doctor?"

She shook her head and tears sprang to her eyes. She didn't bother brushing them away. They were real, though not for the reason he likely assumed. Her life had crumbled around her and now she had no idea what she was walking into with him. Had no idea if she was going to survive this or not. And that was terrifying.

"I don't understand anything that's happened," she cried out. "A man kidnapped me and made me go to Grand Cayman. There was a bank account in my name and I had to close it down. It had millions of dollars in it and now he's got it. He called me all sorts of horrible names and he hates you. He hates you so much." She machine-gunned the words out as she started crying even harder, all the while wondering if Vitaly knew she was lying and was going to kill her right where she sat. But no, he wouldn't want blood in his office, she thought, then bit back another sob at the insanity of all of this.

"Sit, sit." He led her to a nearby chair. "I'm sorry about what you've gone through. Can you tell me about the man?" His tone was quiet, but his blue eyes were ice cold.

Ellis had blue eyes but they were nothing like the man in front of her, the man who didn't care if she lived or died. She swiped at her cheeks. "Why aren't we calling the police?"

He sniffed dismissively. "Of all people you know how useless they are. I don't want them involved in our business."

"But—"

"Enough. I'm not going to discuss it." His gaze drifted down to her wrists and he frowned, lifting one of them up to inspect. "He will pay for what he did." It seemed as if he was saying it more to himself than to her.

Which he was, because he didn't care what happened to her. Vitaly was doing this for himself, because no one crossed him. That was something she saw crystal-clear right now. He would have to make an example of the man who'd taken her—and she would never let him find out it was Ellis Bishop. "I don't understand how there was a bank account in my name with so much money. It's all so bizarre."

"Don't worry about that now. First tell me about the man who took you." He cleared his throat as someone knocked on the door, then told them to go away. As he looked back at her, he said, "How many people were involved with your kidnapping?"

"Only one, really. Well, one that I had to deal with, anyway. I think he worked with others though, because when we went to the bank, he told me someone was inside watching me. But I don't know what they looked like or if they even existed. He could have been lying. We flew down to Grand Cayman and back with the same pilot and he didn't seem to care that the man was holding a gun on me." She and Ellis had gone over the details multiple times and they were embedded into her brain.

It still felt bizarre to be lying even though she knew her life depended on it. Shuddering, she wrapped her arms around herself, hoping she was convincing. She was certainly scared and she didn't have to fake that. Her heart was a wild, out of control mess and she was just glad there was no way Vitaly could hear it.

"You're doing good. Now let's start at the beginning."

So she did, weaving a tale about how a man had taken her from her house even though it had really been from her AA meeting. From there she told her stepfather how this stranger had roughed her up and then made her get on a private plane at gunpoint, how he'd said all sorts of vile things about Vitaly and what a bad man he was.

"He said," her voice cracked as she neared the end of her tale, "that you wouldn't pay a ransom for me, that you were worthless. I thought he was going to kill me!" she sobbed out.

Vitaly pulled her into an awkward hug, patting her back a couple times. "He lied to you. I was negotiating with him, trying to figure out who he was. A few of my associates have recently had their adult children kidnapped. Just like you."

She blinked in surprise at this bold lie, though she wasn't sure why she should be surprised. It was clear he was a master liar and manipulator. Heck, maybe it was the truth, but she doubted it. He was simply trying to explain away why he'd tossed her aside like garbage. "Really?"

"Yes. It's why I wanted to handle this myself without any law enforcement. They just muck things up, as you know. Now, do you know why he let you go?" He watched her carefully.

She shook her head and wiped away the lingering wetness on her cheeks. Vitaly, the jackass, hadn't even offered her a tissue or anything but she kept that thought to herself. "No. But he did say that just because you were a monster didn't mean he was. I thought he was lying though, when he said he was going to call the police to find me. I thought he was just taking me somewhere to kill me."

Vitaly's gaze went distant for a long moment as he stepped back, mulling over her words. "I want you to describe this man to me." Her stepfather leaned against his desk, crossing his arms over his massive chest.

"He wore a mask and baggy clothes most of the time, but he had a beard and I'm pretty sure he's white. Because he didn't wear gloves the whole time." Arianna kept her description vague enough so that it would line up with any potential security videos her stepfather might find.

He nodded once, his expression thoughtful. "In the picture he sent of you, your clothing was ripped."

She cleared her throat and looked down, clasping her fingers together. He wasn't asking a question directly, but she knew what he wanted to know. "He didn't rape me, if that's what you want to know. He ripped my dress and I thought...he would." She cleared her throat, looking away as if she couldn't bear to say it. "He grabbed my... But then he stopped and told me that he wasn't a monster like you." She looked up at him. "Who is this man, and what does he want with you? He hated you. I might not know much, but I feel like this is personal."

He flicked his wrist once in a dismissive gesture. "I have a lot of enemies, which is natural as I am successful. I will find out who this is and take care of him the way I took care of that stupid boy in college." His icy eyes flared with anger for a moment before his neutral mask slid seamlessly back into place. But she'd seen that anger, seen the violence lurking.

And she couldn't pretend not to know what he meant.

When she didn't respond he lifted an eyebrow. "Is there something you want to ask me?" It almost sounded like a challenge.

She swallowed hard. "Yes and no. I don't think I want the answer."

Sighing, he pushed up off the desk and went over to his minibar, pouring himself a vodka on ice. "Your mother told me that she alluded to you what I had done."

Arianna shoved out a breath. She'd always wondered if her mother had told him. When her mom had been on her deathbed she'd told Arianna that her stepfather had taken care of Charlie. And Arianna had been able to figure out easily what her mama had meant. Vitaly had either killed Charlie or had someone do it for him. The carjacking had been in a quiet part of town that saw little violence, the car had been found abandoned not far from the area, and Charlie hadn't been robbed of his wallet or expensive watch. "Did you do it yourself?" she whispered.

He looked over from the bar, a flicker of surprise probably that she had asked at all. He shook his head and took a drink. "You have had a rough couple of days. I think you need to rest. I'm going to get some pictures together and see if any of them look familiar. I know you said he wore a mask, but maybe something will look familiar to you. The pictures might trigger something."

Though she wanted to leave his estate, she knew that would arouse suspicion so she simply nodded and stood. "I'm pretty hungry too. And I want to call my sponsor."

He nodded. "Yes, yes, head to the kitchen. Mario is working today. I brought him with me from Orlando. He will fix you anything you want. You can call your sponsor later. Do not tell her what happened. And *no* police."

"I understand." More than he realized.

As she reached the door, she paused as he spoke. "Arianna, I think it goes without saying that you will never discuss with anyone else what your mother told you."

"I haven't said anything to anyone ever. Why would I tell anyone now? I'm not sorry he's dead." That was the truth too. When he'd died so violently, she'd been relieved for it. Even through the dark haze of all her drinking, she'd been so glad that the monster had been gone from her life. Her glee had actually scared her, made her question what type of person she was. But she'd been spared living through a trial and all the public speculation about whether she'd "wanted it" or not. *Ugh.*

Another flicker of surprise, but then he nodded and dismissed her. As if she was some random employee and not his stepdaughter who'd just supposedly been through a frightening ordeal.

As she stepped out into the hall, she realized that she had absolutely no guilt about helping Ellis. Vitaly deserved to go to jail and Ellis deserved his life back. Ellis was an honorable, wonderful man who shouldn't have to pay for someone else's crimes.

She needed to contact him quickly before he lost his mind. Because she had a feeling that if he didn't hear from her, he would send the police here.

CHAPTER TWENTY-ONE

Arianna turned on the water in the shower of the en suite, leaving it cold so it wouldn't steam up the room as she fished out the burner cell phone Ellis had given her. He'd wanted her to have a way to contact him in an emergency so she'd tucked it into her bra. After what had happened in the parking lot, she knew he was likely going out of his mind wondering what had happened to her. She hated that she'd had to spend time talking to her stepfather at all.

With trembling fingers, she used the hidden camera detector app he'd installed for her and checked the bathroom. She didn't think Vitaly had cameras in here but she was going to be extra careful. Once she felt secure, she punched in the phone number Ellis had made her memorize. It was his emergency burner phone he was only using for her and other trusted contacts.

"It's me," she said as soon as he picked up. "And I'm okay." She kept her voice pitched low, not whispering because that would carry more. "I'm in a bathroom and the shower is running. It should drown out my voice."

"Are you sure you're okay? I checked the tracking app and see you're at his Orlando estate."

Relief slid through her at hearing his deep, steady voice. He'd also installed a tracking app on her secret

217

phone, something she was grateful for. "I'm fine." For now. "What happened to the detective?"

"Carlito got held up at an accident. A motorcycle smashed into the back of a moving truck right in front of him while he was at a red light." Ellis cursed softly. "He couldn't leave the guy to die."

She could understand that. "Okay. So far there seem to be a decent amount of men here. No one is paying me much attention."

"What did he say to you?"

"Mainly he had a lot of questions and he wants me to look at some pictures later. I told him I didn't see the face of the man who took me—I stuck to what we practiced. He's still insisting."

"Good, good." He let out a relieved sigh. "When can you get out of there?"

"I don't know. I've supposedly just been through a trauma. He doesn't want me to leave and I'm not going to push back right now. Not yet, anyway. He also..." She cleared her throat. "He also basically admitted to killing the man who raped me in college. Not himself, but he was behind it."

Ellis sucked in a sharp breath. "I don't know if I like that he admitted that to you."

She didn't think she did either. "I think it was to make sure I understood to keep my mouth shut about the kidnapping and the bank accounts. Which he skimmed right over, refusing to talk about. He might as well have patted my hair and told me not to worry my pretty little head."

Ellis snorted. "I'm working with a contact on my end. I'm going to figure things out. I'm just glad that you're okay for now. But you really need to get out of there."

"I know." She was trying to figure out a reason she needed to leave, but couldn't come up with anything yet. "What are you working on?"

"That video I told you about, the one of Vitaly killing Carter. The guy who took the video has to have a backup. There's no way he got rid of that evidence. He's going to be treating it like his insurance. So I'm working with someone, trying to figure out where he might have stashed a video, whether online or in a physical location. I'm sure he's got both, but I'm going to be looking for the physical location because it'll be easier for me to access."

That was good. Really good. "Listen, I have an idea. I know you're not going to like it, but hear me out. Since I have the cell phone, I can just leave it in my stepfather's office and you can use it as a recorder, basically kind of like a makeshift listening device—"

"No way. You're not doing that."

"Why not?"

"You're not putting yourself in more danger!"

"I won't be. He won't know it's mine if he finds it. And he won't. He's been in and out of there with his guys, so you might hear something you can use."

"No." There was no give to his voice.

She was silent for a long moment. He couldn't stop her. "Just answer the phone if I call you. I've been in here too long, I've got to go."

He let out another curse. "Check in with me as soon as you can. Two hours?"

"Okay. I will. Stay safe," she murmured.

"You too. And if I don't hear from you, I'm sending the police there."

She wasn't sure if he was kidding or not. There was so much she wanted to say to him but she felt weird and tongue-tied. Still... "I miss you," she murmured.

"I miss you too." There was a note of agony in his voice that she felt to her core. "And I hate that you're there."

"I know. Hearing your voice makes me feel better." And it did, which was crazy. He wasn't here, but just talking to him made her feel grounded. Less alone.

Once they ended the call, she felt...bereft. Hollow. No surprise, she missed Ellis. Missed him so much more than she ever could have imagined. That man was in her blood now. She wanted out of this whole mess, wanted him to get his life back.

Arianna's heart skipped a beat as she stepped out into the guest bedroom her stepfather had put her in. Otto was standing in the doorway, frowning at her.

"Who were you talking to?" He stepped farther into the room, looking around as if searching for someone.

She gave him what she hoped was a confused look. "No one. Well, other than myself."

He kept staring at her, his expression unreadable.

Lead filled her gut. What if he suspected something and decided to search her? She cleared her throat.

"Sometimes I talk through things out loud. It's something I learned in therapy. I know it's kind of weird, but it's a good coping mechanism. I talk through my worries."

The tension in his shoulders eased. "Talking therapy. Sounds like something you millennials do."

She wasn't even sure she fell into the millennial category, but she loathed the obnoxious catchall term. Still, she gave him a self-deprecating smile to really sell it. "Yeah. So is everything okay?" Because he had to have a reason to be in her room.

"Yeah. Your stepfather wants you to look at some pictures."

She nodded and fell in step with him, her shoes quiet along the Persian rug runner of the long hallway. This place might not be a mansion like his home in Orlando but it was definitely expansive. She couldn't help but wonder what her mother had ever seen in Vitaly. Yeah he was good-looking and rich and... Okay, maybe that was it.

Her mom had grown up the daughter of poor immigrants from Cuba and she'd married a wealthy Ukrainian man as soon as she'd turned nineteen—Arianna's biological father, who she didn't remember because he'd died when she was four. But according to her mother, he had taken good care of her and had loved both of them. Arianna had no idea if that was true, but it was a narrative her mom had pushed on her frequently. Unfortunately, when he'd died his financials had been a mess and he hadn't provided for her mom as well as she'd thought he would. So she'd married Vitaly years later.

And gotten pregnant almost immediately, something Arianna was sure was intentional. Once she'd "given" him a son—eye roll—Vitaly had given her mom anything she wanted. As far as Arianna knew he had never cheated, though she had a feeling her mother would have looked the other way regardless. Her mother had liked her lifestyle, liked being secure financially. *Ugh.* Arianna pushed those thoughts back down as she normally did. She'd loved her mom, but she'd also been aware of exactly who she'd been.

She wasn't sure why she was thinking about her mother right now. It wasn't going to help her stay focused on the situation at hand.

And right now her life depended on it.

Her heart was in her throat as she stepped into her stepfather's office. If he found out that she'd lied to him…

"I take it you got some rest?" he asked even as he motioned for her to sit down.

Okay, he was acting fairly normal, so maybe he didn't know anything.

"Yes, thank you. Ah, what is this?" She looked at the spread of photographs in front of her. A bunch of them looked like mug shots.

"I'm trying to figure out who took you," he said as if that was obvious.

She tapped a fingernail on the image closest to her. "How did you get mug shots?"

"That doesn't matter. Now take a look at these. And I have a few more once you're done." He motioned to a stack of photographs on the right side of the massive oak desk.

"Okay." Fighting off a tremble, she picked up the first one, shook her head and set it down. She looked at the second one, a white man with a beard, and according to the information on the paper, he was six feet tall. She shrugged, then looked up at Vitaly who was watching her expectantly. "I had a hood on most of the time, and if I didn't, he was wearing a creepy mask. I really won't be able to tell you much. I...never thought about it but the beard might not have even been real. I can say 'maybe' about pretty much any of these guys," she said, sweeping her hand along the desk at the mug shots.

Jaw tight, he simply nodded and turned to speak quietly to Otto who was hovering nearby.

Curious, she picked up the other stack of photographs—which weren't mug shots, but regular pictures. Some had been taken from a distance as if with a long-range camera. She started flipping through them and nearly froze when she saw a photograph of Ellis Bishop. But she didn't pause, instead kept going until the end. Oh God, so Ellis was a suspect too. Which made sense, but she hated that his picture was in this pile. There weren't names or any other identifying information other than the pictures themselves. When she looked up, her step-father was watching her closely.

"Anything?"

"I wish I could be more helpful. Trust me, I wish I knew who the man was." She rubbed at her wrists, hoping to take attention away from her face. She was lying her ass off and terrified he'd see right through her.

Vitaly's gaze strayed down to her bruised wrists, his frown deepening. "We will find out who did this." His phone buzzed in his pocket and he took the call, turning away from her. Easily dismissing her, he held a finger up to her even as another man stepped into the office and started talking in low tones to Vitaly. She'd noticed since she'd arrived that this place was a hotbed of random people she'd never seen before. Which could mean nothing. This could be just what his normal life was like for him. She had no idea. When she'd lived with him years ago, and her mother had been alive, there hadn't been so many people in and out of their home. She wondered if he'd done his business somewhere else.

He stepped out of the office as he spoke to the newcomer, even while telling whoever was on the other end of the phone to hold on in that commanding voice.

She looked around the office, not seeing anything out of the ordinary. Just bookshelves and photographs. Mainly of Max and Vitaly.

Arianna got up from her chair and strode over to a favorite picture of her brother. Smiling to herself she picked it up, her heart twisting at the sight of him laughing. He'd been twelve years old in the picture. Vitaly hadn't been with them that day, but her mom had taken this at the beach. Max had been laughing at some random guy juggling, of all things. That day had been filled with ice cream, sun, sand and laughter. Sighing, she wondered if Max had known what Vitaly was as he'd grown older. She really hoped not and she hated that she couldn't ask him.

The one thing Arianna knew for certain was that Max had loved her. He'd been younger than her but they'd met up for breakfast weekly, had gone to pretty much every local festival together, and had talked on the phone every other day. Yes, his love for her had been real, just as hers had been. You couldn't fake that. Unfortunately he'd had a problem with drugs, one he'd never gotten under control. She hated that she could relate, that her alcoholism would always be a part of her. Maybe it was something in their genes.

Now that she knew Vitaly sold drugs, it was like a sucker punch straight to her gut. A surge of anger streaked through her as she remembered how Max had looked on the floor of the kitchen, vomit at the corner of his mouth, his face an unearthly gray. She hated that it was her last memory of him—hated that he was gone at all.

Glancing over her shoulder, she reached into her bra and pulled the burner phone out. It was set to silent so she didn't have to worry about it buzzing or ringing. She knew it was a risk, but she decided to take it. Ellis had been in hiding for months and so far he wasn't seeing much traction on proving his innocence. She refused to lose someone else she cared about. Not when she could

do something about it. Quickly she used the hidden camera app and when she didn't find anything, she called Ellis.

"You okay?" Ellis asked quietly, not saying her name.
He'd told her that he would never say her name across
this line.

"I'm in his office. I'm leaving this line open."

"No! Don't do this," he hissed out.

Ignoring him, she found the perfect hiding spot on
the top ledge of the bookshelf. There was a fine layer of
dust which told her it hadn't been dusted in a while—
probably because Vitaly didn't even let the cleaning staff
in here. She knew him; he was meticulous about privacy
in his office in Orlando as well. So why would his Miami
one be different? And she couldn't imagine that he would
have cameras in here—because a camera system could be
hacked and it would give anyone who was smart enough
an opportunity to eavesdrop on him. No, Vitaly
wouldn't risk it.

"I'm putting it up now. Don't hang up. I'll get another
cell phone," she murmured. Despite his protests, she set
it on the top shelf out of sight just as she heard the door
open. This would have to be good enough.

Heart in her throat, she turned to find Vitaly stepping
inside even as she smoothly plucked a framed photo up.

He frowned at her but then his expression softened
ever so slightly when he saw what was in her hand. "I
miss Maximus every day."

She wondered if he really did, considering he was
about to flood the streets of Miami with a new designer

drug. But she nodded, not having to fake her emotion at all when it came to her little brother. "I know. Me too. It's silly, but I miss getting bagels with him. Every time I pass that Einstein's, I think of him."

"I'm glad you're okay," he said, shutting the door behind him.

Yeah, only because now he could find out who knew about his offshore accounts. "Me too. I'm still confused about everything. And..." She looked over the stack of pictures. "Do you really have that many enemies?"

He made a dismissive sound as he rounded his desk and sat down. "No, I just wanted to be thorough."

"I understand. Look, I don't have a cell phone and I haven't been able to check in with my sponsor or any of my friends..."

"Oh, of course. I'll make sure you get one."

"I can buy one. I just need a ride—"

"No, no. I will provide you with one. Don't worry about it. For now you need to stay here and rest. I'm working on a business deal, and after everything you've been through I don't like the thought of you being away from me."

She hated the idea of staying here but there was no logical reason for her to argue with him. Especially after she'd just been kidnapped. "How long do you think I'll need to stay here? I need to go to an AA meeting for sure, I need to check in with the woman I'm sponsoring, and I've got plans with some of my friends from school, so—"

"Arianna, I can't give you a time frame. Just stay put and be thankful that you are alive." He spoke as if his word was law, as if he was God. Which sounded about right where he was concerned.

Sensing that she was about to push too much, she nodded. "You're right. If you could get me a cell phone though, I really would appreciate it." Not that she would be calling Ellis from that phone—she would never put him in danger like that—but she did want to call her sponsor. And her stepfather already knew about her relationship with Sheila so it wouldn't be putting her in any more danger than she was from simply knowing Arianna.

She left the office, shoving back the wild surge of emotions sparking through her. Her inner voice was telling her to run, run, run.

But she forced herself to take a deep breath. She had no choice but to stay. If she wanted to get out of this alive, she had to act normal, to bide her time until she could get back to Ellis.

But once she left, she was never coming back.

CHAPTER TWENTY-TWO

Ellis cursed as he heard Arianna leaving Vitaly's office. He couldn't believe what she'd done but there was no way to stop her. *Fuuuuuuck.* He wanted to call in a SWAT team and get her out of there but knew that was impossible. Maybe he could call Duarte and ask him to do a wellness check. No, that might arouse even more suspicion and might get the detective killed. Because when he'd called 911 it wasn't as if he'd told them who he'd kidnapped.

He pressed mute on the burner phone and hoped she'd hid that cell phone well. On another one of his burners, he called Lizzy.

"Yeah?"

"Arianna just planted a phone in her stepfather's office." He clenched his jaw.

Lizzy let out a whoop of excitement. "Seriously?"

He scowled "Yes."

"Give me the phone number to the burner."

He rattled off the number. "What are you going to—"

"Dude, it's a phone. I'm going to hack into it and record anything using the microphone. I can hack into the camera too, if it's usable. That's child's play for me."

Just when he thought his skills were passable, he realized how far out of his league Lizzy was when it came to technology. She was on a different playing field. And he was damn glad she was on his side. The techs he worked with could do the same thing—he just hadn't realized how much Lizzy was capable of.

"Look, I'm thinking of reaching out to someone I used to work for. Someone Bird passed over for a promotion. I'm pretty sure some sexism played into it but there's no way to prove that. Anyway, I'm going to ask her to search his work office. She's got access."

Lizzy let out a low whistle. "You really trust her?"

"I don't know who to trust anymore, but yeah. I trust her enough."

Lizzy was quiet for a long moment. "Is it Laura Leonard? The agent you told me about before."

"Yeah."

"I ran her financials. Hers and the other guy you mentioned. She's not great with money and has some credit card debt. But nothing bigger than average. And she's young. No school loans. She rents, so she doesn't even have a mortgage to worry about. Her financials aren't kickass but they're not worrisome either. I don't know if that helps."

He rubbed his temple. At this point he'd done everything he could. "It does help. Thank you."

"All right, I'm on the phone. I can't see anything through the camera but as long as this phone is turned on, I'm recording anything I get from it."

There it was again, that kernel of hope inside him. "I'm good to hang up on it, then?"

"Yep."

He ended that call and continued rubbing his temple. He'd basically had a headache for months. A dull, pulsing throb that simply wouldn't go away—except when he'd been with Arianna. "You think I should reach out to Laura?" Lizzy didn't know her and could be objective in a way he didn't trust himself to be anymore. He'd trusted Bird and look where that had gotten him.

"I don't know how to answer that. I don't know enough about her so there are too many unquantifiable factors right now. If you reach out to her and she's dirty, you risk exposing yourself to even further scrutiny. But it's not like Bird has forgotten about you. You're still a wanted man. Although I don't think they'll be able to link you together with Arianna, if that's what you're asking. And from what I've dug up on the woman, she doesn't have any skeletons in her closet. No hidden accounts that I can find."

At least that was something. "Thanks."

"No worries. I'm going to keep working on this, see if I get anything good."

"Lizzy, you don't need to do this. I know you have a job."

"I do but I took some time off when you called—"

"What?"

"You gonna tell me to stop doing what I'm doing? Look, I'm still working on some stuff at the office but none of it is critical. Your *life* is critical. Besides, I own stock in the company now. No one's gonna mess with me anyway."

His throat grew tight. "Thank you. I owe you."

She shrugged it off with a grunt. "We're good, trust me."

He half-smiled. "You know my number if you get anything from the recording. I think I'm going to reach out to my former coworker." He had to start making more progress on clearing his name. And he couldn't depend on Lizzy to do everything in her power to help. He knew he'd made progress but it still felt like everything was moving at a glacial pace. And he wanted his life back—now more than ever.

"All right. I'll keep an eye on her communications once you talk to her. Talk to you soon."

After they disconnected, he grabbed the keys to a car he'd parked a few blocks away. He wasn't going to make this call from his safe house. It had been months since he'd talked to Laura and he just hoped he wasn't making a huge mistake. Because if she turned out to be dirty, well...then he'd know soon enough.

Either way, it shouldn't affect him—unless she managed to track down his burner, and then the DEA tracked him to his safe house.

It was a risk he'd have to take.

* * *

Ellis rubbed the back of his neck as he leaned against the oak tree outside the dog park. No one was around and he was far enough away from his safe house that he felt secure enough making this call. He'd already texted Laura, telling her that he was a friend who needed to talk so hopefully she answered. If Laura did trace it, he'd have enough time to get away from the park. Hopefully.

"Who is this?" she asked on the third ring.

"It's Bishop."

There was a long moment of silence, so long that he checked the phone to see if she was still there.

"Bishop. Where are you? No, don't answer that. I don't want to know. How are you?" Through the line he heard the sound of a door shutting quietly.

"I'm okay. Are you tracing this call?" He heard more doors shutting, then opening.

"No. I should though. I'm in the ladies' room at work. I'm checking the stalls now..." Another door opened and shut. "All right, I'm alone. Why are you calling?"

"I need to ask you a favor. Like, huge. I didn't kill Carter."

"I never thought you did." There was conviction in her words that soothed something in him. Her belief in him was probably the only reason she was talking to him now instead of flat out hanging up on him.

"I know who killed him. I saw it. I recorded it."

"Holy shit, then why didn't you turn that over!" she whisper-shouted.

"What I'm going to tell you could put you in danger. Tell me now if you want to know who killed him. Because someone from the administration is involved with the cover-up of Carter's murder. I'm not going to tell you who unless you want to know. Because you will be putting yourself in danger with the knowledge." He waited, letting her decide.

It didn't take her long. "Just tell me. We all loved Carter. I don't like the way your case was handled and I really don't like how neat and tidy that whole murder scene was. It never sat right with me—or a lot of people. Tell me what you got."

"Vitaly Rodin killed Carter. Shot him point-blank. I got it on my cell phone and gave it to Kyle Bird. But not before I emailed a copy to myself. He confiscated the phone and erased my accounts and sold me out. He's working with Vitaly and I guarantee he's using the video as leverage against the man."

A long silence dragged out between them. "That's quite an accusation," she finally whispered.

"I know. And I also know that Bird has backup copies. He has to, otherwise he's a complete moron. And he's most definitely not or he wouldn't have lasted so long as a goddamn traitor." Ellis took a deep breath, shoving back his rage every time he thought of Bird, of what the man had covered up and stolen from him. Of how he'd killed Carter.

"Jeez, Bishop. This is…"

"I know. It's why I asked you if you wanted the details. I can't be certain, but I wouldn't be surprised if he had a backup copy of the video in his office. It's more secure than any bank or deposit box."

"I…I can't get involved. I've got to go." She hung up on him.

Well, then. Sighing, he rubbed a hand over his face then shoved off the tree. He needed to get out of here in case she decided to run a trace on him. He'd thought that with her history with Bird passing her up for a promotion, she might be open to listening to him.

Apparently not.

CHAPTER TWENTY-THREE

After he talked to Laura, Ellis kept questioning his decision to reach out to her, but it was done now. And he'd gotten his answer—she wasn't helping him. Not that he should be surprised. He was asking her to risk a lot, the least of which was her career.

Though he didn't like leaving the vicinity of his safe house, Ellis needed to grab some more burner phones from one of his stash locations. And while he was there, he loaded up on some canned goods and other food.

By the time he got back to his safe house, he was even edgier and feeling out of control—because he hadn't talked to Arianna. He hadn't heard from Lizzy though, so he knew she must be okay. Or he could only hope she was. The not knowing was eating him up inside and giving him irrational thoughts.

Stupid thoughts.

Like storming Vitaly's estate and getting Arianna.

But that would just get himself, and possibly her, killed.

Damn it. He had to get Arianna out of that house and give her a good reason to stay away from Vitaly's estate. One that Vitaly would be okay with. Because otherwise she'd just have to go on the run with Ellis. But the first step was simply getting her away from Vitaly, especially since she'd planted that damn phone.

He'd been running over different ideas in his mind and could only come up with one halfway decent one. One that her stepfather wouldn't question. But there were some logistics surrounding it he'd have to smooth out first. Even then, it was only a temporary fix.

As he opened the door from the garage into the kitchen, he froze for all of a second before he withdrew his weapon. The alarm hadn't gone off for him to disengage.

"Don't shoot!" his sister's familiar voice called out.

Evie...

Heart still racing, he sheathed his weapon and pulled the door shut behind him. On silent feet he walked through the house and stopped in the living room, surprised when he found that Evie wasn't alone.

Lizzy set her laptop on the coffee table and rounded the long dark blue couch. Wordlessly she pulled him into a big hug. At five feet eight or nine, she was fairly tall for a woman and her grip was hard despite her slender frame. She'd cut her hair since he'd last seen her. Now the dark brown barely hit her shoulders. But she still had the same sense of humor, if her T-shirt was any indication. Today it read, *This is what genius looks like* and she had on sparkly purple Converse sneakers to complete the look. "It's good to see you, even if you do look a little like a lumberjack."

He laughed, the sound rusty as he hugged her back. "What are you guys doing here?" There was no way they'd showed up without having something important to tell him. His stomach lurched. "Is Arianna okay?"

"She's fine. Well, as far as I know she's fine. But you're going to want to listen to this."

When he didn't move fast enough, Evie grabbed him by the upper arm and basically shoved him into a sitting position on the couch.

Lizzy tapped a few buttons and then a recording popped up on her laptop. She pressed play.

"I say we start next week. Hit the Keys all the way up to Orlando in one swoop. Not a ton, but a trickle of what's to come." Ellis recognized the voice of Vitaly's second-in-command, Zach Foster.

"It's very soon after…the power shift."

Okay, so they were sort of talking in code. But it was pretty clear that Zach wanted to release drugs along the East Coast of Florida next week. And Vitaly wasn't so sure about doing it so soon after his boss had been murdered.

There was a slight shuffling sound, then what sounded like liquid being poured. Okay, someone was getting a drink. "You need to strike hard and fast now. You've already made it clear that you're the boss. No one's going to challenge you, not now. We've been hoarding our product for months. And the red, white and blue crew are ready to meet tomorrow."

"I know." There was a faint sound, as if someone was tapping a finger against the desk. "I don't like what happened with Arianna," Vitaly finally said.

Zach made a scoffing sound. "Someone has a vendetta against you. This isn't news."

"I don't like being blindsided when I'm about to launch a new product. The timing doesn't sit right."

The man was very careful with his words, Ellis would give him that.

"Look, I've got feelers out on the street. No one is talking because everyone is too terrified to cross you."

"Not everyone, clearly. My instinct says it was the Boy Scout."

He lifted an eyebrow, wondering if that was a reference to him. Evie always called him that, as did people at work. Ellis's frown deepened.

"We leaked the info about Arianna to the Boy Scout's former CI—he said he told the Boy Scout." Clothing rustled.

"I know. I want to tie up that loose end—and I'd planned to when he came for her. She says she was taken from her house. So either your guys were slacking—"

"No way. The Boy Scout is good, clearly. Or he wouldn't be alive still. If it was him who took her—and I'm not convinced it was—then he would have come in through the back and been quiet about it. It's not like we were able to sit on the house 24/7, and her phone has a tracker so it wasn't important anyway."

"Maybe."

"No, definitely. Why do you think it was him?"

"She wasn't assaulted. Not really. She said he just roughed her up a little but didn't rape her. Anyone else on my list...they'd have hurt her badly. And he let her go instead of killing her when I wouldn't meet with him.

That narrows down my list substantially and he's at the top of it now."

"Whoever it is, I will find out who took her and then you can make an example of him. We can't miss this opportunity. Besides, you've got your people on the inside. We'll be able to meet with the crew and get what we need with no pig interference."

The pig reference was clear too. Disgust filled Ellis as he listened to the rest of their conversation. It was mostly benign stuff but it was very clear that Vitaly planned a big meeting tomorrow and that his concern wasn't for Arianna, but whether she now was a threat to him.

"What is the red, white and blue crew?" Evie asked as the recording ended.

"He's talking about the Dominicans. He's been working with them a lot in the last six months without the knowledge of Berezin. They've been cutting side deals, running weapons but mainly drugs. Berezin had a falling out with the Dominicans but Vitaly kept up his link with their leader. Now it's clear why. And his man on the inside has to be my former boss. Bird's going to help him get away with flooding the streets with drugs and look the other way. He'll make sure their meeting goes off without any interruption." That level of corruption and betrayal enraged him.

"Tomorrow could be a chance to catch Vitaly in action," Evie said. "Maybe Bird too. And if you can get Bird, you know he'll flip on Vitaly to save his own skin. He'll give up that video if they give him a sweet enough deal.

Then you'll clear your name. And even if he doesn't flip on Vitaly, all his credibility will go out the window if he gets brought down. This could be good for you no matter what. You'll be able to build a case against both of them and make sure you're in secure holding."

She was right. Still... "I only trust a couple people at the DEA right now and none of them could run a sting operation at the last minute. And we don't have the manpower to set something up."

His sister crossed her arms over her chest. "Well, I might have a solution for that. But you're not going to like it."

"Say it."

"I trust the Fed who was in charge of Evan's bombing case."

"Georgina Lewis." He knew the woman.

"I think we should bring her into this. It puts you in danger of being arrested. But we can't turn away from this opportunity. You can get your life back. I think it's worth the risk to tell her what we know, but it's not my life."

Nodding, he stood, pacing. Evie was right. He couldn't sit on the sidelines and do nothing when this might be his only opportunity. Even if they busted Vitaly tomorrow, it didn't guarantee any change for Ellis's situation, but it would bring Vitaly down. And the bastard deserved it after killing Carter.

"If I go along with this, if we reach out to the Feds, I need to get Arianna out of Vitaly's house. Immediately."

As in ten minutes ago. Once he was in Fed custody, he wouldn't be able to help her anymore.

A low-grade buzz hummed through him at the knowledge that she was still there, under that monster's roof. An angry swarm of bees were stuck inside him, stinging, stinging, telling him that if he didn't get her out soon, she wouldn't last. And he couldn't stand the thought of a world without her in it. *No.*

"I agree. I don't like her being there," Evie said.

"I have a plan to get her out," he looked at Lizzy, "but I'm going to need your hacking skills."

Lizzy nodded once. "Just tell me what you need."

CHAPTER TWENTY-FOUR

Arianna took a bite of the oatmeal she'd made, but it might as well have been sawdust. She couldn't taste anything as she sat at the island countertop in her step-father's kitchen. She'd barely slept at all last night, wondering if he was going to find that cell phone. And even if he did, would he be able to trace it back to her? She couldn't see how, but still. It would look suspicious and something told her that he wouldn't hold back from questioning her—or worse.

She mustered up a half-smile as Otto strode into the kitchen. He grabbed a banana from the bowl on the island. "How are you doing? You look kind of pale. Are you sick?"

"I'm good enough." She picked up her coffee mug, needing to keep her hands busy with something. Dammit, she needed out of this house.

Run, run, run. The words repeated over and over in her head. Because deep down she knew that if she stayed, she was going to die. Or maybe that was just the panic she was letting invade all the blank spaces inside her. And even if she did leave, she wasn't sure where she'd go. If she went anywhere other than her home, it would look suspicious to Vitaly. Still, she wanted space from him.

Her new cell phone Vitaly had given her buzzed in her pocket and she jerked, sloshing a few drops of dark coffee onto the pristine marble countertop.

She was sure it had some sort of tracking app or spyware on it like before. But she'd been able to transfer all of her old numbers and information to this one from her online backup, so she'd reached out to the woman she sponsored to apologize for being MIA.

"Is that your phone?" Otto asked.

"Yeah."

She didn't make a move to get it, but when he stared at her expectantly, she fished it out and glanced at the screen. It wasn't like she thought Ellis would actually contact her on her phone but she was letting her nerves get the best of her.

Her stomach tightened when she read the message from her sponsor, Sheila.

In the hospital. I'm okay but came down with the flu. It turned into pneumonia. They're pumping me full of fluids. I won't be at any meetings this week. I'm in room 243 if you want to stop by. Would love to see a friendly face. Bring chocolate.

The message was kind of formal but she imagined that it probably had taken all of her friend's energy to type out the message anyway. She shoved back her chair, leaving her half-eaten bowl of what was now mush.

"What is it?" Otto asked.

She tucked her phone into her back pocket. "My friend—ah, my sponsor," she added because it wasn't a secret to her stepfather or Otto that she was a recovering alcoholic. "She's in the hospital. I have to go see her."

Otto shook his head even as he tossed the banana peel into the trash. "You're not supposed to leave the house."

Anger intermingled with fear inside her. Who was he to tell her what she could or could not do? "Whoever kidnapped me let me go. He apparently got what he wanted and that doesn't include me anymore. I'm going, so unless you plan on kidnapping me too, I'm gone."

Otto cursed behind her as she hurried out of the room. She wasn't familiar with this house but she knew that various sets of car keys were on a hook right outside the door that led to the garage. And if she couldn't take one of those cars, she would simply call an Uber.

"Wait," Otto said as he hurried after her, typing something into his phone.

"You're not stopping me." The truth was, he could totally stop her if he wanted but she wasn't sure that was how her stepfather wanted to play this. She could be wrong though. Maybe he was going to go all heavy-handed and keep her a prisoner.

"I'll drive you," he said as they reached the door to the five-car garage.

She turned to look at him in surprise. "You don't have to."

"Yes, I do."

Oh, that meant her stepfather had ordered him to. She didn't like having an escort but she would take it.

With the way Otto drove, it thankfully didn't take long to get to the hospital.

She texted Sheila, letting her know that she'd arrived. In response, Arianna received a happy face emoji.

After stopping by the information desk for directions, they headed to the bank of elevators on the first floor. This place was huge, and if they hadn't been given directions, she would have definitely gotten lost.

"Look, you don't need to go inside with me. Not right now. She's got pneumonia," she said as Otto pressed the correct floor on the elevator pad. "I want to see how she's doing first."

"All right. I'll grab some coffee in the cafeteria, but I'm not leaving."

"Thank you."

"Want me to grab anything for you?" he asked as she got off on the right floor. He put his hand out to hold the door open instead of following her.

"I'm okay. I've got my phone on me if you need me." Heart racing, she hurried down the hallway, following the signs. It was quiet on this floor, which had to be a good thing for Sheila. She couldn't believe her friend had gotten the flu so quickly. And pneumonia on top of that. Arianna knew Sheila had been so looking forward to having coffee with her daughter and she hoped that it had gone well.

As she reached the correct door, she knocked softly and pushed it open a few inches. She didn't want her friend to have to get up.

"It's me," she called out. "I don't have any presents, because I wanted to get here as soon as I could. I'll grab you anything you want from the cafeteria though." Quietly, she eased the door shut behind her. The bed was empty but the bathroom door was closed so she must be in there.

As she stepped farther into the room, Ellis and a woman she recognized stepped out of the bathroom.

Arianna's eyes widened even as joy filled her to see him.

"Are you alone?" he murmured.

She shook her head. "One of my stepfather's men came with me. He's in the cafeteria though."

Evie hurried past her to lock the door.

She wasn't sure what the heck was going on but she rushed toward Ellis at the same time he moved toward her. He hauled her to him, his grip tight, and she hugged him right back. God, she'd missed him and they hadn't been apart a full day. He smelled like the Irish Spring soap he used, but underlying it was that masculine scent that drove her crazy.

"I needed you out of the house. A friend of mine cloned your friend Sheila's phone. She's completely fine. No flu."

She let out a shaky breath and shifted back so she could look up at him. "That was pretty risky."

"I know. But something is going down tonight and I can't do anything unless I know you're safe."

"Tonight? With my stepfather?" She glanced over at his sister, who'd remained quiet.

Ellis hesitated. "Yes. I'm meeting up with the Feds today. I want to help bring Vitaly and my former boss down. I don't know how things will work out. They might arrest me. I just don't know."

"You're not going to be arrested," Evie snapped.

Ellis simply shrugged and kept his gaze pinned on Arianna. "I don't know anything at this point, but I couldn't move forward until I knew you were safe."

"I've missed you," she whispered, holding on tight. It was weird having an audience but she didn't care.

"I've missed you too," he groaned as he bent down, barely skating his lips over hers. It wasn't nearly enough but she understood. She wasn't going to make out with him in front of his sister because that was beyond weird, and they were both still in danger with Otto nearby.

"So what happens now? Now that I'm out of the house? You're going to the Feds and...what will I do?"

"I wasn't sure if you would have an escort or not. If you ditch him it will look weird and put Vitaly on alert—which could screw up tonight's meeting."

"So you're just going to stay here," Evie said, drawing Arianna's attention to her.

"What do you mean?"

"I mean you'll hang tight in this room with me. You can tell your stepfather's guy to go home. If he doesn't want to, he doesn't have to. But I have a feeling that if you make a big enough stink about him wanting you to leave, you'll be fine. I doubt he's going to pull a gun on you and drag you out of here."

True enough. Unless he was completely stupid, they'd catch him on camera. "What about the hospital though? They're not going to let us just hang out here."

Evie snorted. "Our parents donated an entire wing. One of the doctors—who is friends with our dad—is handling a 'patient' in here who is famous and wants their privacy. All nurses have strict instructions to stay out. This room is ours. Trust me, we're totally fine right now. If anyone comes in, I'll be posing as said famous person's assistant and tell them to get lost."

Oh, right. She forgot that Ellis came from a whole lot of money. Ellis was so grounded it was easy to forget.

"Just listen to whatever my sister says." He leaned down and kissed Arianna, harder this time.

She kissed him back, swallowing all the questions she had as she put her feelings, her hunger, into this kiss. She knew now wasn't the time to grill him, could feel the energy and tension pumping through Ellis as if it was a tangible thing. He'd taken a risk by getting her out of her stepfather's house and she would totally listen to his sister.

"Just be safe," she ordered as he pulled back.

"You too," he rasped out.

* * *

Tension hummed in Ellis's chest as he stood in the driveway in front of his brother Evan's truck.

"She won't throw you to the wolves," Evan said as if he'd read Ellis's mind.

Ellis rubbed a hand over the back of his neck, not making a move for the walkway yet. He couldn't order his feet into action. "I don't have a lot of faith in people lately."

"Well you better have faith in me and Evie. And I'm telling you, Agent Lewis—Georgina—is solid. You know that or you wouldn't be here."

"Yeah, I know. It doesn't mean I have to like it." He'd left Arianna in the very capable hands of his sister and he trusted Evie more than most. He trusted his brother too, but Arianna would feel safer with Evie.

And if he was being honest, if someone came after Arianna, he trusted Evie to slit their throat if necessary. Evan was also capable, but Evie, she had that killer instinct. Not to mention that she was a woman, so people would naturally underestimate her. His sister would use that to her advantage right before she struck someone down with a vicious blow they never saw coming.

"Don't think I'm going to forget that you brought Evie into this before me," his older brother muttered. Evan had a beard now, and though it covered most of the scars on the side of his face, those pinkish lines and striations dipped down lower, past his neckline. The scars aside, Evan was different now, more serious.

For some reason the ridiculous words made him laugh. "I sent you a postcard before her."

His brother just grunted. "Were you referring to kidnapping when you said you had things figured out?"

Ellis just shrugged.

Evan shook his head. "Why did it come from Montana?"

"I used a company that mails postcards from random places for a fee. Look, I've missed you guys. I mean, I know I've been on undercover work forever anyway, but this is different. I *couldn't* come home." But he'd wanted to.

Taking him off guard, Evan grabbed him and pulled him into a hug. "We've missed you too."

He squeezed back then took a step back, shoving the knot of emotion down into his chest. There was no time to process that now. "Let's do this."

All his muscles were pulled taut as he strode up the walkway with his brother toward the nondescript house in a quiet neighborhood of one-story ranch-style homes. Before he could knock, Agent Georgina Lewis opened the door.

In jeans and a long-sleeved dark blue sweater, she stepped back. Her dark hair was pulled up into a ponytail and her gray eyes popped against her brown skin. And her expression brooked no bullshit. "Come on in. It seems we have a lot to discuss."

Even though the back of his neck tingled, telling him it was stupid to jump into the fire with federal agents who could arrest him at any moment, he nodded and walked straight into the lion's den. At least his brother had his back and he knew Arianna was safe.

Knowing that made everything else easier to deal with.

He was going to do what he came here to do—confirm to the Feds about Vitaly and Bird and about the recording of Carter's murder.

Evie had already talked to Georgina and given her the recording taken from Vitaly's office, or the woman wouldn't even be meeting with Ellis.

Now, he just hoped they finished things and took down Vitaly and Bird. And that Carter finally got the justice he deserved.

CHAPTER TWENTY-FIVE

Arianna stretched her legs out on the bench by the hospital window. As far as rooms went, this place was impressive. The floors were some kind of faux wood in a light coloring, the bed looked larger than normal, and the three-panel window let in a lot of natural light even with the tint over the glass. Everything was in tones of cream and gray but was soothing more than depressing. The Bishop family really must have friends here. And if they'd donated a wing, no wonder.

She and Evie had chatted throughout the day, though Evie had been working on her cell phone and laptop on and off. Arianna wanted to know if her calls had anything to do with Ellis, but anytime she asked a question about what was happening tonight Evie had shut her down. Not that she blamed her.

Even now, Evie was pacing by the door, talking in low tones to whoever she was on the phone with. After a growl of frustration, she suddenly shoved her phone into her pocket.

"Is that about Ellis? I mean, I know you can't tell me any details, but is he okay?" Arianna could hear the desperation in her own voice but didn't care.

Evie's blue eyes narrowed ever so slightly. "You really do care about him."

256 | KATIE REUS

"I do." So much that it scared her. Especially now, knowing that he might end up in jail.

"Good." Sighing, his sister absently tugged on her long, dark ponytail. "He's fine. I just want to be there with him tonight."

"With him? Is he…working with the Feds, like directly?" He'd been so vague and Evie hadn't been any clearer.

Evie lifted a shoulder.

Okay, that was answer enough. Shutting her eyes, Arianna rubbed her temples. Her phone buzzed, pulling her out of her own thoughts. "It's Otto. He's ready to go." And it was no wonder, considering it was almost six o'clock. She texted him back, telling him that she was going to stay and that he could leave.

She frowned at the next text.

I'm on my way up.

"Crap," she muttered, swinging her legs off the side of the bench. "He's coming up here. Let me head this off and tell him to go home."

"If anything feels off just come back here," Evie said.

"I will." Arianna knew the other woman didn't like letting her leave but she'd met with Otto a few times throughout the day just to check in with him so he didn't get nosy and come up here—and find that she was in a room with Evie Bishop, sister of her stepfather's enemy.

"In fact, here, take this." Evie handed her a folded-up knife.

She stared at it. "What do you want me to do with this?"

"Stab somebody."

She snorted. "That's not happening."

Evie shrugged. "Just hold on to it. It'll make me feel better knowing you're armed."

Even though she had no intention of using a knife, Arianna took it and tucked it into her pocket. Unless she physically opened it, there was no chance of it accidentally popping open and stabbing her. And since Evie was Ellis's sister, she didn't want to insult her by rejecting it.

"So...you think the whole eating Fritos plain thing is weird, right?" she asked, hoping to lighten the mood and take her mind off everything.

"Oh my gosh, yes!" Evie nodded enthusiastically as they headed to the door. "It's the grossest thing. I mean I like Fritos and chili, but by themselves? No thanks. Ellis is such a weirdo."

Arianna half-smiled as she reached the door. "I'll be back in five or ten minutes. Depends on how long it takes me to convince him to leave." She had a feeling she had an argument on her hands, but she didn't care. No way was she going back to that house.

"I'm going to tail you, but I'll stay out of sight."

She nodded and stepped out into the hallway, looking both ways before taking a right and heading to the elevators. She hoped to cut Otto off before he even made it to this floor.

Her sneakers were quiet as she strode down the mostly deserted hallway. It had been quiet all day, and Evie had told her it was because it was a recovery wing.

Which was good because she hadn't had to deal with seeing anybody. Apparently they'd worked some sort of magic and the room was off-limits to staff as well.

When she didn't see Otto, she got onto the elevator and texted him that she was on her way down to the lobby. Stepping out, she found him focusing on his phone, his brow furrowed as he looked at the screen.

"Hey, you can just go ahead and leave. I'm going to hang out for a while since she doesn't have any family local. I can Uber back to my stepdad's."

Frowning, Otto tucked his phone away. "No, you're coming back to his place. I have strict orders."

He paused as a man wearing pale blue scrubs stepped out of another elevator. The guy didn't even seem to see them, just kept looking at something on his phone as he hurried down the hallway.

Arianna shoved her hands in her pockets to hide her trembling. "I don't care what your orders are. I don't work for my stepfather and I'm staying here."

Surprising her, Otto snaked out a hand, grabbing her upper arm in a viselike grip. "No. You're coming with me."

The first frisson of fear slid down her spine as she looked into his cold eyes. Gone was the nice man she'd known before, the one who told her she reminded him of his own daughter. Now she was looking into the eyes of a cold-blooded criminal who worked for her stepfather. "I'm not going anywhere," she gritted out, tugging against his grip.

"Yes, you are." He tightened his fingers hard enough to leave a bruise. "And you have some explaining to do."

She tugged again, trying to step away from him. "Explaining?" Oh, God, had they found the hidden cell phone?

"Yes. I just talked to your stepfather. It seems your friend isn't at the hospital at all, but up north visiting family."

Arianna hid her reaction, frowning at him. Evie had told her that her hacker friend had somehow managed to ping Sheila's phone so that it appeared as if it was in Miami. "You're out of your mind. She's just upstairs."

He pulled a gun out of nowhere and shoved it into her ribs. "Save the bullshit."

She sucked in a breath but he cut her off.

"Scream and I shoot the next doctor or orderly who comes down this hallway," he snarled as he started dragging her down the connecting hallway. Arianna had no choice but to comply, fear all but choking her.

They'd barely gone a few feet before he pushed on an exit door.

No no no. This was happening too fast. Evie wouldn't know what had happened to her.

"Your stepfather has some stuff to handle tonight, but then he's going to deal with you. And whoever is up in that room, if there is anyone, will be dealt with soon enough too." There was far too much glee in his voice.

Another burst of fear exploded inside her at the thought of Evie being up there by herself, alone and vulnerable.

Lifting her elbow, she tried to strike out at Otto but he backhanded her across the face. Stars exploded behind her eyes as her head snapped back.

Her cheek throbbed as she stumbled forward, the pain stunning her.

"Try that again and I'll knock your teeth out." His voice was ice-cold as they reached a waiting SUV.

He shoved her into the back, following in after her as he pulled out flex ties.

Fear gripped her throat as he secured them to her wrists and ordered the driver to move. Did they know about Ellis? About Evie helping them? Nausea swept through her, but she pushed it back down. If she threw up on herself, it wouldn't matter and she knew Otto would make her sit in it.

So she gritted her teeth, praying that Ellis was okay and that somehow she'd figure out a way to escape. The first opportunity that presented itself, she was running.

CHAPTER TWENTY-SIX

Ellis sat on a fishing charter boat about two hundred yards from the coastline, within viewing distance of the warehouse where Vitaly was supposed to meet the Dominicans.

After Carter's murder, the Feds had picked up the investigation, and while they'd been hunting Ellis, they'd also been looking into the possibility of a different murderer. Apparently Bird was already on their radar, which gave Ellis back some of his faith in the system.

Georgina had explained to him that she and a team had started digging into Bird after two men—who had broken into Ellis's house while he'd been on the run—had been killed in federal custody. There was no way the killer had gotten a weapon on the transport without help. And all the FBI's digging had led them back to Bird. From there, they'd started investigating him. Hard.

So combined with the information Ellis had given them, they knew where this meeting was tonight. Ellis had been vague on how he'd gotten a recording of Vitaly and his second, and they hadn't pushed too much. The Feds wanted to bring down Bird and Vitaly—and they were gunning for Bird since he was a dirty DEA agent. But taking down Vitaly's operation and taking out a traitor would look good for the FBI. Really good. And those things mattered when it came time to get funding. Agent

Lewis refused to let Ellis take part in the real op, which he definitely understood. He was a liability, considering he was currently wanted for murder.

But she had him under official supervision with one of her guys and they were on the periphery of the op, posing as fishermen while keeping an eye out for when the Dominicans arrived. The boat itself was registered to a real fisherman who was part of the FBI's cache of informants.

The agent, who'd told Ellis to call him Teddy—whether that was his first name or a nickname, Ellis had no clue—tapped his earpiece. "We're quiet on this end. What's up?" He listened in silence, though he glanced over at Ellis more than once. And his expression was far too neutral.

Shit. Was this it? Were they going to slap the cuffs on him and haul him in now? Maybe Vitaly had canceled the meeting and the Feds were going to cut their losses and arrest Ellis for real. Arresting him would sure look good for the Bureau, and he hated that he was cynical—and experienced—enough to expect it.

Jaw tight, he glanced out over the water rippling under the bright moonlight. It was good conditions for night fishing and they weren't the only boat in the bay—which only helped with their cover. Still, no sign of the Dominicans.

When his phone buzzed in his back pocket, he snagged it immediately. Only a couple people had this number, including Arianna. He'd been forcing himself not to think about her—obsess was more like it—and failing. He kept telling himself that if he could just get through tonight, just get through one more day, he'd be that much closer to bringing Vitaly down, getting justice for Carter—and starting a life with Arianna as a free man.

A lead ball congealed in his gut as he read his sister's text.

I took out two guys at the hospital. They have A. Tried to follow but they got away in an SUV. The plate's a fake, but it's one of V's men. I don't know where she is, couldn't follow. Phone off. Can't track. Heading to V's estate now to check if she's there.

He wanted to ask her what had happened but it didn't matter. *Arianna has been taken.*

He had to get out of here, had to get her back. *No, no, no.* How had this happened?

"There's been a change in our situation." The agent's voice cut through his thoughts of jumping out of the boat and swimming to land and trying to hunt her down. It was a stupid plan with no chance of success, but Ellis needed to find her.

"What?" he asked, trying to keep his shit together.

The guy looked slightly uneasy. "Georgina just let me know that your friend has been taken. It appears as if Vitaly has the woman on-site. She arrived in an SUV under guard."

Though it took self-control, he didn't look in the direction of the warehouse in case they were being watched by Vitaly's men. Instead he tossed out a line, pretending to continue fishing even as his mind whirled.

"Arianna is there now? You're sure?" he demanded.

Teddy nodded. "In the warehouse inside one of the SUVs. I'm just giving you a heads-up. Our team will do everything to make sure she comes out of this okay."

Not good enough. He shot off a text to Evie telling her to sit tight and not bother going to Vitaly's house because Arianna wasn't there. No, she was in far more danger right now. "I want an earpiece." At least he knew where Arianna was and that she was alive, but knowing it didn't make him feel any better. She would be directly in the line of fire when the Feds raided the warehouse.

If Ellis had ever thought he knew what fear was, he'd never truly experienced it until that moment.

The agent's jaw tightened then he spoke quietly to whom Ellis assumed was Georgina, since she was in charge of everything.

"All right." Teddy fished a small earpiece out of his windbreaker jacket pocket and handed it to Ellis. "Keep quiet. Don't interrupt anything."

He nodded, knowing they were giving him a professional courtesy he shouldn't be getting, considering the circumstances. So he wasn't going to be a dick about it and interrupt anything.

As he forced himself not to look in the direction of the warehouse, he couldn't help but question whether he should have turned himself in earlier or not. If he had, he wouldn't have met Arianna, but she wouldn't be in this position.

She'd be at home, safe, far away from all this. Now it was too late and her life was on the line—and there was no way for him to get to her.

CHAPTER TWENTY-SEVEN

With her hands still bound, Arianna wiped her damp palms on her pants as the driver of the SUV got out and shut the door behind him. Unfortunately Otto stayed right where he was beside her.

Inside a brightly lit warehouse there were far too many sketchy-looking men standing around. She knew they were near the water because Otto hadn't blindfolded her on the drive here.

In fact, he didn't seem to care if she saw anything. And he hadn't taken his gun off her the entire time. She had a bad feeling she wasn't getting out of this alive. At that thought she had to wipe her palms down again.

She was still holding out hope for Evie, however, because Otto hadn't been able to get a hold of whoever he'd sent up to the hospital room.

When her door was wrenched open, Arianna flinched to see Vitaly standing there. God, she'd been so wrapped up in her head that she hadn't realized he'd approached.

There was no warmth in his eyes, just rage.

She flew forward as Otto shoved her, grabbing onto the door with her tied-up wrists. She barely stopped herself from falling onto the concrete.

"Otto," her stepfather snapped. "That is enough."

Arianna steeled herself for whatever came next and faced him.

"What were you doing in the hospital?" Vitaly demanded, jumping right to it.

Not answering, she turned her head as a man strode up to them. She vaguely recognized him. He was white, maybe in his fifties, seemed to be in good shape...

Then it clicked. This was Ellis's former boss, Kyle Bird. She looked away from him, not wanting either of them to see any recognition on her expression. And she wasn't a great liar.

Pain exploded in the left side of her face as Vitaly slapped her with an open palm. It stung, shocking her in its abrupt violence. The sound was loud, echoing in the warehouse as everyone else went still and quiet including Bird and Otto. Zach was there as well, her stepfather's right-hand man, but he was off a ways by one of the rolling doors as if waiting for someone.

A stinging heat spread across her cheek as she turned to stare at Vitaly.

"I won't ask again." His words were quiet, his tone deadly, and a shiver ripped down her spine.

Before she could say a word, Otto stepped up next to her. "We should cancel tonight. If she's talked to the Feds we need to be smart."

Bird snorted. "Please. If there was going to be a sting operation, I would know about it. There's no one in the vicinity watching us. I have all of my people in place. This will go off smoothly. I wouldn't be here otherwise," he snapped out the last part forcefully.

Vitaly didn't respond to either of them but stayed focused on Arianna, clearly watching for a reaction.

Thinking fast, she said, "A man named Ellis Bishop kidnapped me. He hates you. I never lied about that. But I did help him," she spat at her stepfather, unable to hide her rage. She had to be somewhat truthful right now or they would call off this whole meeting. Considering what Ellis had told her, she now understood that her stepfather was going to get busted tonight. Maybe soon. She couldn't let him leave, because if the Feds were going to bring him down this would be the place it happened. So telling him half-truths would hopefully keep him in place—and get him busted by the Feds.

Vitaly's eyes narrowed. "You helped a man who kidnapped you?" His tone was slightly mocking.

"Not at first, you murderer! But he told me what you're like—showed me how awful you are. You opened that account in my name and you run drugs. Drugs! I can't believe that after everything that happened to Max. You should be ashamed of yourself!" She screamed the last part. "He's dead and you put that same garbage on the streets." She didn't have to fake any of this as all the fear bubbling under the surface came out in a rage. She hated Vitaly, hated everything he stood for and that he'd stolen Ellis's life.

Sighing as if she were a nuisance, Vitaly turned to look at Bird. "Would your former employee kidnap a woman?"

The man lifted a shoulder. "Yes." Then Bird looked at her. "Is that what this is all about? Why were you at the hospital?"

Vitaly held up a hand, his expensive watch glinting under the harsh lights of the warehouse. "Don't speak to her," he said, though his focus was still on her. "But you will answer the question, Arianna."

She stuck out her chin defiantly. "He wanted me out of your house because you're a horrible human. He loves me," she added, hoping she sounded naïve enough for him to dismiss her completely. "He wanted to know what you'd talked to me about and to make sure I was okay. He's going to be leaving the country soon and wanted to see me, to ask me to go with him."

Vitaly's mouth curved up ever so slightly. Which was basically his version of a laugh. "You really are a stupid little girl." He looked at Otto. "Keep her in the SUV. I'll take care of her later. She has nothing to do with tonight."

"Like I said," Bird muttered, "if someone wanted to storm this place they would have done it right now, considering you have a kidnapped woman." As if to reiterate he started talking to someone, through an earpiece she guessed, then spoke to Vitaly again. "The perimeter is clear."

Vitaly's eyebrows rose slightly, then he nodded. At least this time Otto didn't shove her, just ordered her to get back into the SUV.

She did, praying hard that Vitaly got what was coming to him tonight before she ran out of time. And she prayed that she made it out of this alive. If she did, she was going to tell Ellis how she felt. She didn't care if it was too soon. She loved him. Simple as that.

Fighting tears as they sat there, Arianna wasn't sure how much time passed as they waited for...something. Through the tinted window she watched Vitaly making phone calls, his expression staying neutral except for brief flashes of annoyance. If there had been a chance to escape, she would have taken it by now, but she was completely surrounded. The only thing she could hope for was that the Feds would save her.

When a big bay door rolled open and a speedboat zoomed into a docking station, everyone seemed to jump to attention. A taut energy filled the place, even in the interior of the SUV where it was just her and Otto, who had moved to the driver's seat. At least she didn't have to sit next to him anymore.

The speedboat was all sleek and slender and she had no doubt that thing flew across the water at crazy speeds. If she had to guess, it was for running drugs.

Vitaly approached as three men exited the boat while one stayed on board. The one on board waved off one of Vitaly's men when he tried to tie the boat off and the two seemed to be going back and forth about that. She couldn't hear anything from where she was and it wasn't like Otto was talking to her.

"Does your daughter know what you do for a living?" Arianna couldn't keep the disgust out of her voice.

She'd clearly startled Otto because he jerked ever so slightly, barely glancing over his shoulder at her. "I paid for her college and she is happy."

"I'm sure she would be *so* proud of you. A big, tough man who roughs up a third-grade teacher."

His jaw ticked and she knew she'd struck a nerve. She probably shouldn't be baiting him but she didn't care because *screw him.* If she was going to die, she was going to be as loud and obnoxious as possible until the end.

"When did you see her last? No answer?" she continued. "Maybe at the next family get-together you can tell her you helped kill an innocent woman. I'm sure that'll earn you her undying respect."

"Shut your mouth."

Uh, no. "I wonder if the reason she moved so far away was to get away from you because she knows what you are." Over the years Otto had shown Arianna pictures of his daughter and they were all when she was younger, the oldest being as a teenager. She'd never thought about it before but why didn't he have any older pictures of his daughter?

Otto slammed his fist down on the center console and started to turn toward her when suddenly all hell broke loose.

She reared back in shock as men and women with blue windbreakers and a whole lot of guns stormed the warehouse from the main door, and some even rappelled from the rafters like freaking ninjas.

Heart in her throat, she ducked low as gunfire erupted everywhere.

Otto jumped from the vehicle so she pulled her knife out of her pocket and started sawing away at her wrist ties. It didn't take long to get free even as she tried to ignore the *rat a tat tat* of the gunfire outside.

Ping. Ping. Ping.

The SUV rang with each bullet that smashed into it. She was pretty sure the only reason she was still alive was because the thing had to be bulletproof. A weird numbness had spread across her entire body and she wondered if she was in shock. No, she'd know if she was, right? She had to be though. It was the only reason she wasn't having a complete breakdown.

Suddenly her door yanked open. For a brief moment relief punched into her because she thought it was the FBI coming to save her.

But it was Vitaly who grabbed her, his blue eyes wild and angry—and fearful. She'd never seen fear before from him. His entire body trembled as he shouted, "Get back!" Dragging her in front of him as if she was a rag doll, he used her as a shield.

She started to struggle until he pressed a pistol to her head.

Icy talons sliced down her back, fear carving deep into her. She wasn't getting out of this alive. No, screw that. She was going to survive this.

As he dragged her backward, she kept her knife tucked into her hands, not that it would do her a lot of good right now. Even if she managed to lift the knife up, Vitaly would shoot her before she could stab him. And she did not want to die. No, she wanted to live, with a desperation she'd never felt before.

Years ago when she'd been at her darkest, she'd wondered who would care if she was gone, if it would even matter. Now she had Ellis and she wanted to live to see him again. To tell him what he meant to her. So she kept her knife down low out of Vitaly's sight. If she ever got the opportunity, she was going to use it.

"Drop your weapon!" A woman with brown skin and piercing gray eyes waved at other federal agents to put their weapons down.

Out of the corner of her eye, Arianna saw that Vitaly's men and the Dominicans were lying on their stomachs. Some were shouting angrily but most were allowing themselves to be handcuffed. It also looked as if three men were dead, including Otto. Unfortunately Vitaly had managed to save himself. He really was a slimy bastard.

Instead of responding, Vitaly continued walking backward toward the boat.

"I'll dump her offshore, unharmed. But I will kill her if you come any closer." His voice echoed loudly.

Liar. He would never let her go. He was going to kill her.

Arianna could see the indecision in the female agent's gaze as she kept her weapon pinned on them. But from her position there was no way she could actually hit Vitaly without endangering Arianna too.

"Step to the left," Vitaly ordered Arianna.

That was when Arianna realized they'd made it to the boat. The driver from before was in the water, facedown, clearly dead. She did as he ordered, conscious of the gun still pressed to her head.

Staying low and out of the line of sight, he snapped at her. "Put it in reverse."

Swallowing hard against the sudden rush of bile, Arianna kicked the boat into reverse, nearly stumbling when the powerful machine revved to life.

It shot backward out into the open water. And as soon as they were clear, she knew Vitaly would shoot her in the head and dump her.

CHAPTER TWENTY-EIGHT

Ellis knew he wasn't supposed to have a weapon but—"Give me your backup pistol!"

Teddy didn't even give him a sideways glance, but to Ellis's surprise he reached into his holster and gave him a pistol.

Well, hell. He must have gotten prior approval from Agent Lewis. That was the only thing that made sense.

"Do *not* let the target into open water," Agent Lewis's voice said across the comm line. "He must not be allowed to escape."

The order wasn't for him, but for the agent.

Water splashed everywhere as they slammed into a cluster of small waves. "Faster, faster," he demanded as they raced across the water toward the Donzi speedboat. It ate up the distance but not fast enough as they crashed into another wave. The other boat hadn't even reached max speed. Not even close.

The sleek and slender Donzi shot toward them like an arrow, glinting white under the moonlight. Ellis could hear Georgina ordering someone to call the Coast Guard but he didn't care. It would be too late by the time the Coast Guard got to the boat. Vitaly would have killed Arianna by then.

Not on his watch.

As the Donzi swerved erratically and slowed down, he realized Arianna was driving—probably because Vitaly was staying low and hoping he wouldn't get shot by the FBI.

"Ram them!" Ellis shouted above the rumbling engine. It was the only way they'd stop the other boat. The Donzi was too fast, able to max out at almost ninety miles per hour if they allowed it, and would outrun any boats they sent after them. No, they had to stop them now when they were going slow enough. He hated the risk to Arianna but it might be the only way to save her.

Teddy didn't respond as the speedboat continued racing toward them. Instead, the agent swerved hard, the bow ramming right into the hull of the Donzi.

Ellis launched backward under the impact, slamming into the side of the boat as the Donzi jerked, then stilled. Arianna tumbled out of sight as the Donzi thrust backward into the air. It was a miracle the thing didn't flip. Instead it crashed back against the water, sending an outward wave in all directions.

"Stay back!" Teddy shouted as he maneuvered the boat up next to the idling Donzi.

Ignoring him, Ellis propelled himself over the side and dove onto the other boat. Pain ricocheted through him as he slammed against the hard fiberglass on his hands and knees. As he shoved up, he whipped out the pistol.

On his knees, Vitaly had Arianna by the hair and was holding her in front of him as she struggled to stay upright against the slick bottom of the boat. The man's eyes were wild and angry as he brandished his pistol around in the air.

He knew what he was doing though—it wasn't madness that Ellis saw, but rage. Anger that he had been outsmarted, that he was going to jail. No matter what, he wasn't coming out of this unscathed and the bastard knew it.

Ellis just hoped he didn't try to take Arianna with him. He couldn't— God, no, he couldn't even go there. "Put the weapon down. They'll go a lot easier on you if you don't hurt her." He forced the words past his tight throat. He had to keep his shit together if he wanted to save Arianna. Save the woman he loved.

And love her he did. No doubt about it.

"You lie," Vitaly snarled even as out of the corner of his eye, Ellis saw Arianna pulling something out of her pocket.

He had to keep the other man talking. *Just keep him talking.* The longer Vitaly was talking, the longer his focus wasn't on her. Though it took all his self-control, Ellis didn't look at Arianna's face. He simply couldn't. If he saw the terror and fear he knew must be on her expression, it would rip him apart and he'd lose focus. She needed him now and he wouldn't fail her.

"You know what I did, and Bird will turn on me in exchange for leniency. This is Florida. I'll get the needle." Vitaly's weapon wavered as he started to point it at Ellis instead of Arianna.

In that moment, she slashed down and Ellis saw the flash of a sharp blade as it arced toward Vitaly.

Vitaly screamed, falling back as she slammed the knife into his thigh.

Ellis used the momentum to fly at him even as Arianna dove away from Vitaly. He knew the other agent was behind him, but nothing mattered other than getting Vitaly far away from Arianna.

His whole body shook under the impact as he body-slammed Vitaly—just as the cold steel of the man's pistol pressed against his side.

Without pause, Ellis pulled the trigger of his own pistol.

CHAPTER TWENTY-NINE

Arianna screamed as the gunshot filled the air. Pushing up, she crawled her way to Ellis, but hard hands clasped her shoulders.

In a panic, she swung out but a man caught her fist in his hand solidly. "It's okay. I'm the FBI." He gently took her knife away.

Barely hearing him, she shoved his hands off her and turned, fighting the terror threatening to choke her. "Ellis!"

Everything fell away as Ellis stood, tucking a pistol into the back of his pants as he faced her. Sharp relief punched through her as if she'd been physically struck. He was alive. He'd shot Vitaly, who now lay unmoving, his eyes staring sightlessly as a dark stain spread across the front of his shirt.

Wordlessly she launched herself at Ellis, fighting the sob bubbling up.

"Are you injured?" His deep voice penetrated the fog in her mind as he gripped her shoulders and stood back, his gaze sweeping over her from head to toe.

"I'm fine. Are you okay?"

In response, he hugged her close, burying his face against her neck.

"Oh my God, your sister—"

"She's okay. She took out the threat," he whispered in her ear.

Before she had time to react, the man who'd been driving the other boat and claimed to be with the FBI placed a gentle hand on her upper arm. "Ma'am, you need to come with us."

Suddenly there were more agents on another boat arriving and the rest of the world crashed in on them like a tsunami. The boat dipped as a wave smashed against it. She clutched onto the side as a man wearing an FBI jacket took Ellis from her and slapped handcuffs on his wrists.

"Hey! What are you doing!" she shouted, ready to launch herself at them.

"It's okay," Ellis said. "I knew this was going to happen. This is standard protocol. Please go with them. You're safe." His voice was calm and steady as he nodded for her to go with the agent who was trying to talk to her.

She stared in horror as he was led onto another boat. She wanted to scream and rail against the federal agents but knew that wouldn't do any good. So somehow she kept her cool and allowed the agent to guide her onto one of the Feds' boats.

As soon as she got onto dry land, she was calling a lawyer. No way was Ellis being punished for any of this. If they thought he'd serve any jail time, they were about to feel all of her wrath.

CHAPTER THIRTY

Ellis paced back and forth in the interrogation room. He'd been there for the better part of six hours and though they had taken his handcuffs off, he wasn't free. Not even close. The door was locked—he knew because he'd tried the handle. And no one had come back to see him for the last hour. All he wanted was to talk to Arianna, or at least for some news on her. She'd looked shell-shocked as he'd been led away and he had to make sure she was okay.

When the door swung open and Agent Lewis strode in, her expression neutral, he wasn't sure what to think.

"Come with me," she said, leaving the door open. The woman looked exhausted, but not angry.

Frowning, he did as she said, stepping out into the narrow hallway with her. They strode down to a bank of elevators where she used her key card, but she still didn't say anything.

A few minutes later they were in an office that was most definitely hers. Sparse, save for a few family photos and a wall full of plaques.

"You are officially free to go," she said as she motioned for him to sit down. "But I wanted to talk to you before you left."

Stunned, he sank into the green chair in front of her desk. It squeaked as he leaned back. "I'm free? Bird flipped on Vitaly?" Not that it would do him a ton of good, considering Vitaly was dead.

The look Georgina gave him was practically feral. "Oh, he tried, but someone anonymously sent me the video of Vitaly killing Carter, so he had nothing to give me. Our techs have already viewed it and it's real. Since we have evidence that Vitaly Rodin killed Carter Watson, you have officially been cleared of any wrongdoing."

He wasn't sure why he was being let go because he'd still kidnapped Arianna—and he'd admitted to it. He'd done it to clear his name, sure, but he'd broken the law. And the Feds wouldn't let him go no matter what. "But Arianna—"

"Ms. Stavish is denying that you kidnapped her. In fact, I believe her exact words were, 'Maybe that fool hit his head on the boat, because he's wrong. I would know if I'd been kidnapped.' Then she went on to wonder if perhaps someone in the FBI had roughed you up and forced a false confession out of you." She cleared her throat, her mouth twitching slightly. "She might have even used words like 'FBI brutality' and started shouting at everyone to let her see you before she sued our asses off."

Ellis stared across the desk at the highly decorated agent. "She said I didn't kidnap her?"

"That is correct. And I haven't put your statement into our database yet. So I highly suggest you change your original statement to match hers. Off the record, of course, that is my suggestion." She cleared her throat. "Look. Vitaly killed Carter. He's dead, so we can't punish him, but we're breaking apart his entire organization right now. You had your life taken from you. You deserve this break, so take it. *No one* wants to see you arrested. We already have a huge smear on the DEA with Bird's treachery. Well, his and others. It's a giant mess that we're trying to unravel right now. So arresting you will only make things worse, and my boss doesn't want to deal with even more shit.

"*On* the record," Georgina continued, "thank you for helping us bring down this organization. You're going to be named in the report as an integral part of the op. And I'm ninety-nine percent sure you're going to get a fat promotion and raise after everything you've been through. You'll get stationed anywhere you want. DC, if you ask for it."

He didn't want a promotion, and if they offered it, he wasn't going to take it, but he wasn't going to tell her that. She wasn't his boss and this wasn't his agency. And frankly, he gave zero fucks about the DEA right now. Besides, Lizzy had already offered him a job at Red Stone Security and he was pretty sure he'd take it. None of that mattered now, however. "Where's Arianna?" he demanded.

"She's here, a few offices down. And before you ask, she is also free to go. She's done nothing wrong and we know that her stepfather used someone to open those accounts in her name. We've already started seizing all those assets, including that check from the Grand Cayman account, and for the record, she is not a person of interest. Nor do we expect her to be. And for an elementary school teacher, she's tough as nails." She let out a little laugh. "Maybe *because* she's a teacher. Now come on." Georgina stood and he followed suit.

He felt as if he was on autopilot, being ordered about, but he followed the agent and jerked to a surprised halt as she opened the door to another office and he found his whole family standing there.

His mother, tall and beautiful, with a worried expression, rushed at him. She threw her arms around his neck and squeezed so tight she stole his breath. "My baby," she sobbed.

He couldn't remember the last time he'd seen her cry so he held her tight, his gaze connecting with Arianna, who was slowly inching closer to the door even if there was a soft smile on her face. But there was also a distance in her expression that he didn't like.

"I'm okay. All the charges have been dropped." He'd barely taken a breath before he was tackle-hugged by his father. Closing his eyes, he hugged his dad tight.

For so long he hadn't been sure he'd see his family ever again. And definitely not under happy circumstances. To be here with them now, to be free again...it was almost too much to digest.

As he finally stepped back, he immediately pulled Arianna into his arms. "I know what you said to the Feds," he whispered.

"I wasn't letting you go to jail for something you didn't do."

"Well I did kidnap you," he murmured.

"I beg to differ, and I don't remember it that way. I think you really did hit your head." Her tone was tart even though she whispered it low enough for his ears only as his family talked among themselves.

"Where were you going?" He kept his voice pitched low. "Because I saw you inching toward the door."

Seeming not to care about their audience, she cupped his face, her eyes wet with tears. "Look, right now you need to be with your family. You've been on the run for months and you're finally free. You deserve to go back to your real life. Your parents and siblings have missed you."

He placed his hands over hers, savoring the way she touched him. "Thank you for all your help. Just...thank you." Arianna had stepped up to help him when she didn't have to—when he'd given her every reason not to.

His throat squeezed as he choked up, unable to find any more words. Thankfully she held him tight and when he finally loosened his grip he was tackle-hugged by his brother. Laughing because he was free, because he felt so damn good, he gripped Evan hard.

Isla and Dylan were there also, both officially part of the family now. He couldn't thank his sister or Dylan enough, but he kept all his words to himself for now. He doubted this room was bugged but he wasn't going to say any more while they were inside a federal agent's office. In fact, he wanted to get out of there, to grab Arianna and his family and go home.

But by the time he finished hugging his family, he realized she'd left.

CHAPTER THIRTY-ONE

Arianna sat at her island countertop drinking coffee, normally one of her favorite things to do, but she barely tasted it. She should be elated that she had her life back, that Ellis was free. That he could go back to his life a free man.

She couldn't help but wonder if it was going to be without her. She would know of course, if she'd stayed with him and his family. But she hadn't wanted him to feel weird last night—or technically this morning, considering he hadn't been let go until two o'clock—so she'd made things easy for him.

But now that she was back in her little home that she loved, with Christmas music playing in the background, she simply felt hollow inside. She missed Ellis, missed everything about him. Maybe she'd made a mistake in leaving, but it had seemed easier at the time. Easier than letting him reject her. God, she hadn't even given him a chance, hadn't told him how she felt. It was pathetic.

Ugh. She was such a coward.

And she really needed to get to an AA meeting. After everything that had happened over the last week, she needed to be surrounded by familiar people. People who knew her struggle. It wasn't like she had the urge to drink right now, but that didn't mean she was going to

forgo meetings. They kept her on the right path, reminded her that she needed to keep living the life she
was. Sighing, she set her mug in the sink and rounded
the countertop only to freeze when she heard a door
shut.

"Arianna? It's me." Ellis's voice carried from somewhere... She hurried out of the kitchen and stepped into
the hallway to find him heading in from the backyard.

Ellis! Her heart sang at just the sight of him. "What
are you doing here? And how did you get in?"

"Your security needs improvement." He handed her a
bag that smelled delicious.

She took it but didn't look inside, instead staring up
at him. She drank in every inch of him, noting that he'd
trimmed his beard a lot. It was neat and tidy and sexy.
And he was watching her with those pale blue eyes she
was constantly getting lost in. "Okay, why are you breaking into my house?" And why was she asking? She was
just happy to see him. She should be stripping him naked
and having her way with him.

"I thought I saw someone hanging around out front.
It looks like a reporter so I decided to sneak in."

"Yeah, I got a few calls so I turned my phone off. Apparently word has spread fast about Vitaly's death."

"Is that why your phone keeps going to voicemail?"
he murmured, his gaze falling on her lips for a moment.

"You called me?"

"Of course I called. I've been calling and texting and
going out of my mind. Why'd you leave this morning?"

Unable to answer or take his scrutiny, she turned and headed back into the kitchen. "There's coffee if you want some." She looked into the bag and saw that he'd brought her a bunch of pastries and a breakfast sandwich. The gesture was sweet, and for some reason it made her want to cry.

"Look at me," he ordered softly, his deep voice wrapping around her in a sensual ribbon.

She abandoned the bag and looked up at him from across the island. "I don't know what to say."

Moving slowly, he stalked toward her like a sleek, sexy panther, pure predator in each step until he stood right in front of her and was impossible to ignore. "Tell me why you left."

"Look, you got torn from your real life for months. I know what we shared was...intense. But we were thrown into circumstances together more or less against our will. I didn't want you to feel awkward or like you owed me anything. So I decided to make it easy for you."

"That's bullshit," he snapped, anger flaring in his eyes. "You are my life now."

She sucked in a breath at his words but she didn't drop her arms from around herself. "Ellis, you don't have to—"

"I know I don't have to say anything. And your excuse is flimsy at best. Why did you leave?"

"I was scared," she blurted. "I haven't been in a real relationship...technically, ever. I dated in college and then...well, then my life got shitty. And I haven't dated anyone in years. Then you come along and blow up my neat and tidy world. And I'm serious. I really don't want you to feel some weird obligation to me. I'm clearly not handling things well. I'm a mess and I'm pretty sure you don't want to hitch your wagon to this." Why was she pushing him away? Why did she always do this?

He snorted and took her hands, forcing her to drop her protective embrace. "The only thing I feel for you is love and a whole lot of lust." He pulled her close then, wrapping his arms around her tightly. She'd missed his scent, his hold—him—so much. Even if she'd wanted to move, she couldn't have. "I love you."

"Ellis…"

"What? I do love you. So much."

Oh God. She loved him too. Her throat tightened as she shoved back that annoying bitch in her head telling her she had no idea what she was doing, that she wasn't cut out for relationships. "I love you too. And I was a coward before. Your whole family was there and it was just a lot to take in. I felt like an interloper, like I didn't belong. I shouldn't have run," she whispered.

"As long as you don't ever run again. They all want to get to know you. Especially my mom. She's horrified that I kidnapped you and wanted me to tell you that she did not raise her children to kidnap people. I wish I was joking, but that's practically verbatim." His mouth curved up in amusement.

Arianna let out a startled laugh. "That's good to know."

"Evie already adores you, and you helped me get my life back. Trust me, my family is going to love you more than me soon enough."

A rush of tears sprang to her eyes and she buried her face against his chest for a long moment. It had been so long since she felt part of a family, and even then, it hadn't been strong. She missed her brother and mother deeply, but there had always been cracks and fissures with her mom. And her brother had struggled with drugs so much in those last years. She was so damn afraid to hope that this might be real, that she might get the family she'd always wished for. "You're really and truly free?"

He nodded and hoisted her up onto the center island. She spread her legs so he could shift in closer, heat already pulsing through her at his nearness. She'd missed him with a desperation and it had only been a few hours.

He gently played with a lock of her hair. "It turns out that someone anonymously sent the video to Agent Lewis."

"Lizzy?"

He shook his head. "She ended up finding an address where she's pretty sure Bird stashed a hard copy, but no, it was one of my former coworkers. I reached out to her and she found a backup hidden on his computer at work. I hadn't even thought she was going to help me but...she did."

"She hacked it?"

"No. Apparently she and Bird had a thing ages ago and then he passed her up for a promotion because he didn't want the image of impropriety. It was a whole messy thing, but turns out, she had his password. It took some searching, but she found it buried. She was horrified to learn that he was working with Vitaly so she turned it over anonymously and asked me not to tell anyone it had come from her."

"Are you going to tell anyone?"

He shook his head. "No. It doesn't matter the source and she simply doesn't want to be linked to Bird at all, not even to turn over the incriminating video. It would likely come out how she got his password and then their past relationship would become public. She doesn't want it to ruin her career and I don't blame her."

Arianna nodded, just glad his name had been cleared. "Does it feel weird to be free?"

"Weird, but I'm grateful. And for the record, I think we should move in together." Leaning down, he brushed his mouth over hers oh so tenderly.

Fighting the surge of lust that punched through her, she pressed a hand to his chest. "That's...really soon."

He lifted a shoulder, his mouth curving up in a way that was far too sexy. "I lost too much time so I'm not wasting any more. I want to wake up every morning and see your face—and go down on you."

"Ellis!"

His grin was pure wicked as he kissed her again.

"I'm a Bishop and apparently when we know something's right, we know. So it's not too soon." Then he kissed her hard and everything else faded away as she arched into him.

Even though it scared her, she wanted to live with him too, wanted to take a chance on them. When she'd thought she was going to die, she'd known without a doubt that she loved him. No, she'd known before that. Even if some part of her was afraid of getting her heart broken, Ellis Bishop was definitely worth the risk.

Three months later

Ellis wrapped his arm around Arianna's shoulders and kissed the top of her head, inhaling her sweet vanilla scent.

"This is probably my second-favorite picture from our wedding." Arianna set a framed picture of Evie, Evan, and Ellis next to a picture of him and her on their wedding day.

"Second-favorite?" he murmured, wondering if they could skip their dinner plans with his family and head straight to bed.

"Well, this one is definitely my favorite." She pressed her fingers gently to the framed image of the two of them.

Arianna was in her long, lacy white dress, a crown of little white flowers in her hair and her dark hair blowing in the breeze. They were looking at each other with clear love in their eyes. It hadn't been a posed picture, but a candid shot the photographer had randomly snapped during the festivities.

Ellis looked back at the other picture of him and his siblings and smiled. That one had not been taken by a photographer, but by his mother instead. As he looked at the two pictures, he still couldn't believe he was married.

To the love of his life.

"I'll drink to that." Evie clinked her beer bottle against Evan's.

Ellis added his flute, which held nonalcoholic champagne, to the toast. Arianna didn't care if he drank, but he found himself abstaining more often than not these days.

"Gotcha!" His mother held up her phone triumphantly. "And that's probably the cutest picture I have of my babies."

"Mom!" Evie said in that exasperated way of hers. Ellis had come to learn this was just something that happened between mothers and daughters.

"What? I'm not waiting to get pictures from the photographer. My children all live here again and I'm happy. I won't start harassing you about grandchildren because I know it's your business. But...I'm just letting you know that when or if you are ever ready, your father and I will be more than happy to help out. A lot."

"Duly noted," Evan murmured and Ellis could tell his brother was fighting a smile.

Ellis was also pretty sure that Isla was pregnant, but neither she nor Evan had said anything so Ellis wasn't going to ask. He figured they'd tell everyone when they were ready.

"I'm going to steal your mother for a bit." Ellis's dad swooped in, dragging their mom back to the dance floor.

"You think we'll be like that when we're older?" Evan asked him as Evie laughed at their parents getting down on the dance floor.

"I sure hope so." Ellis's gaze strayed to where his new wife was standing with Isla, Dylan, Lizzy and her husband, Porter.

Arianna was laughing hysterically at something, probably something Lizzy had said because the woman was a smartass.

He owed her so damn much—without her help he wasn't so sure he'd be here today with Arianna.

Ellis was thankful every damn day that he was. After his name had been cleared, he'd taken a job at Red Stone and was working exclusively in Miami for the time being. Not long after that, he'd officially proposed to Arianna—barely a month later—and they'd moved in with each other about two seconds later. He'd wanted to live with her sooner, but she'd wanted to wait until things were more official. So he'd put a ring on her finger.

From there he'd fast-tracked the wedding, much to no one's surprise. And since she and Lizzy had become fast friends once they'd met in person, Lizzy had even been in their wedding, along with Sheila, another one of Arianna's friends, and Isla and Evie.

"Me too. Damn, we really hit the jackpot." *Evan only had eyes for Isla.*

"That's true," *Evie said.* "But don't let Dylan hear you say that. I like to remind him every morning that I am the most awesome thing to ever happen to him."

Ellis snorted. "That man is a saint if he can put up with you."

"Right?" *Evan said.* "We should give that man a medal."

Evie straightened. "Hey!"

"Children, don't make me come between you." *Their mom appeared again and linked arms with Ellis, the joy on her face clear. She patted his arm gently as she leaned up to kiss his cheek.* "I'm so glad you found Arianna. She's such a gem."

"Yes, she is."

As if she knew he was looking at her, Arianna turned and locked gazes with his. It didn't matter what she'd been saying or who she'd been talking to, she broke away and hurried over to him as if he'd called her.

Laughing, his mom released him as he wrapped his arms around his wife and held her close. Ellis didn't think he was ever going to get sick of saying that word. Wife.

"I can't believe how many people are here." Arianna linked her fingers around the back of his neck, her smile wide and infectious.

"I know." It was ridiculously big, but they had a big family and his parents had wanted to invite half of Miami.

Dylan had graciously offered to let them have their wedding on his estate grounds, and the band hadn't let up in the last two hours. The dance floor had been packed for most of it. They'd already cut the cake, done their first dance and had been mingling and thanking everyone for coming. He was ready to leave so they could start their honeymoon early but was forcing himself to be patient. Though he was having a hard time remembering why. Their guests would understand if they left.

"Like, I don't even know who those two people are," she said, motioning to a couple talking to Evie.

"That's Finn and his new wife, Samara. Samara worked with Evie before she married Dylan. And Finn is Dylan's personal doctor."

"Wait, she worked with Evie in that super-secret job you still won't tell me about?" Arianna gently nudged him in the ribs.

He grinned down at her and shrugged. "Why don't you ask her?"

Her eyes widened. "No way. Your sister scares me a little bit. Especially after I found out what she did to those two guys at the hospital."

Ellis smiled, something he was doing a lot of lately. All because of the woman in his arms. He didn't think it was possible *for anybody to be as happy as he was. And now the whole world knew she was his. "Come on, let's show everybody our moves." He scooped her up and hurried to the dance floor, her laughter wrapping around him like the sweetest embrace.*

Even a year ago he couldn't have imagined that this would be his life, that he would've found a woman who eclipsed everyone and everything, and that he would be at his own wedding. Dancing, and happy about it.

He'd been given a second chance in life and he wasn't ever going to take it for granted. And he was never taking Arianna for granted. She was the best thing that had ever happened to him.

She was his North Star. As long as he had her, he would always have a home.

Thank you for reading Bishop's Endgame. I hope you enjoyed the wrap up to this trilogy. I loved writing this group of characters even if I'm a little sad to say goodbye. I also hope you enjoyed the little cameos from some of my Red Stone Security characters! It was fun visiting them again.

ACKNOWLEDGMENTS

Sometimes I feel like a parrot in my acknowledgements because I always thank the same people but I am SO incredibly grateful to each and every one mentioned. Big shout out to Kaylea Cross who read the first draft of this book (as always). I'm so grateful for your insight and friendship. Thank you to Julia for your thorough edits. Sarah, thank you for all you do behind-the-scenes. Jaycee, you know how much I love this cover (and the whole trilogy). I'm also super thankful to all my wonderful, wonderful readers! You are the reason these books are possible. Thank you for your encouraging emails, for buying my books and definitely for talking about them. You guys are the best!

COMPLETE BOOKLIST

Darkness Series
Darkness Awakened
Taste of Darkness
Beyond the Darkness
Hunted by Darkness
Into the Darkness
Saved by Darkness
Guardian of Darkness
Sentinel of Darkness
A Very Dragon Christmas
Darkness Rising

Deadly Ops Series
Targeted
Bound to Danger
Chasing Danger (novella)
Shattered Duty
Edge of Danger
A Covert Affair

Endgame Trilogy
Bishop's Knight
Bishop's Queen
Bishop's Endgame

Moon Shifter Series
Alpha Instinct
Lover's Instinct
Primal Possession
Mating Instinct
His Untamed Desire
Avenger's Heat
Hunter Reborn
Protective Instinct
Dark Protector
A Mate for Christmas

O'Connor Family Series
Merry Christmas, Baby
Tease Me, Baby
It's Me Again, Baby
Mistletoe Me, Baby

Red Stone Security Series®
No One to Trust
Danger Next Door
Fatal Deception
Miami, Mistletoe & Murder
His to Protect
Breaking Her Rules
Protecting His Witness
Sinful Seduction
Under His Protection
Deadly Fallout
Sworn to Protect
Secret Obsession
Love Thy Enemy
Dangerous Protector
Lethal Game

Paranormal Romance
Destined Mate
Protector's Mate
A Jaguar's Kiss
Tempting the Jaguar
Enemy Mine
Heart of the Jaguar

ABOUT THE AUTHOR

Katie Reus is the *New York Times* and *USA Today* bestselling author of the Red Stone Security series, the Darkness series and the Deadly Ops series. She fell in love with romance at a young age thanks to books she pilfered from her mom's stash. Years later she loves reading romance almost as much as she loves writing it.

However, she didn't always know she wanted to be a writer. After changing majors many times, she finally graduated summa cum laude with a degree in psychology. Not long after that she discovered a new love. Writing. She now spends her days writing dark paranormal romance and sexy romantic suspense.

For more information on Katie please visit her website: https://katiereus.com

Made in the USA
Columbia, SC
24 February 2021